PLURIBUS

PLURIBUS

MICHAEL KURLAND

DOUBLEDAY & COMPANY, INC.
GARDEN CITY, NEW YORK
1975

All of the characters in this book
are fictitious, and any resemblance
to actual persons, living or dead,
is purely coincidental.

Library of Congress Cataloging in Publication Data

Kurland, Michael.
Pluribus.

I. Title.
PZ4.K9674Pl [PS3561.U647]   813'.5'4
ISBN 0-385-02925-X
Library of Congress Catalog Card Number 74-12695

For Diane Cleaver

PLURIBUS

~~~~~~~~~~~~~~~~~~

It was a woman had the vision. She was young and newly married, and her husband was impotent and talked a lot about sin.

On Sunday she stood humbly at the back of the church, her black, crackling-stiff cotton dress sheathing her frustration, and told the congregation what the Lord had said to her as she slept. Her blood pulsed heavily through sensitive tissue near her skin while she spoke, and her body moved under her dress and she grew excited with the Word of the Lord.

The congregation listened and grew uncomfortable.

She finished and sat down amid a fidgety silence. Everyone stared straight ahead and waited for someone else to make the comment he wanted to hear.

Every idea has its time.

The next Tuesday, as the preacher suggested, the men met in council to discuss the implications of the Lord's Word. All women, including the visionary, were excluded.

The preacher brought the meeting to order and announced that he didn't feel that he should preside. He turned the chair over to the secular leader of the church council.

Seth Brethenster rapped the gavel a few times gingerly on the table and cleared his throat. "Well," he said, looking around for support, "we all know what we're here t' discuss. Who wants t' say somethin'?"

Outside, several horses neighed nervously.

Seth drummed his fingers on the table and stared into the porridge of scrubbed faces, wondering inconsequentially what common compulsion had caused all but three of the assemblage to show up in their churchgoing suits instead of the coveralls that were weekday garb for both town and farm.

"Harrumph!" Gruber Flynn cleared his throat and looked uncomfortable as everyone turned. "I, ar, we . . ."

"Come on, Gruber," someone called from the security of the mass, "spit it out!"

Gruber ran a finger under his collar and slowly rose, gathering confidence from the rush of words that festering grievance had dammed behind his lips. "We've suffered them weirds up in the enclave too long," he said. "Shit—what kind of teachin' do we expect our kids to follow with that place just sittin' there practicin' the same stuff what brought the Death? And no more 'n ten mile away?"

"He's right!" someone yelled from a back seat. "We owe it to our kids to do somethin'—and it's damn well time we did!"

"Damn right!" Gruber agreed, running his tongue around his dry lips.

A man in black with parchment skin and deep-set, staring eyes arose like coiled spring steel and slowly spread his glare around the room. The coughing stopped and some men held their breath.

"Friend Irad," Seth Brethenster said, nodding to the intense presence.

"My time is not yet come to speak," said Irad, rolling out the words like pebbles in a barrel. "I would but remind you all that we are on the Lord's business, and He will not abide profanity. We must not stain a sacred cause with blaspheming words." He sat.

Seth shook his head in sharp agreement. "Go on, Gruber. But watch your talk—this here's an official meetin' and like Irad says, we'd best not swear."

Gruber's tongue flicked from side to side in his mouth like a nervous hummingbird. "I didn't think," he said. "I suppose I got too riled up. Them people over there, like animals, practicin' that immoral stuff: free love and science, like brought on the Death, and communistics and the Lord knows what else they do up on that hill. And we, God-fearin' folk, just try to teach our kids the meanin' of the Holy Book and avoid the Mistake. I think it's time, high time, that somethin' strong was done. And now that Lucy Siddens had a vision, like the Book says, pointin' the Way and tellin' what the Good Lord wants us folk to do, well, that's good enough for me."

"Now hold!" Tom Barker, the town blacksmith, stood. His hulk-ing muscles strained at the seams of his ancient suit jacket. "I'm just a simple man. I don't claim to know much about . . . any of this. You know I don't have kids of my own; and you all seem to be puttin' this in terms of what's good for the kids. Now I don't think that gettin' vengeful sets a good example for these here kids. The enclave's been up there all our lives, and our fathers' and our grandfathers' since before the Death; and we've been here, and they don't mix with us much nor we with them. Now I don't hold with changin' what has worked till now just on the word of one hysterical woman. If God wants somethin' done, let Him ask me direct."

Someone muttered, "Blasphemy," and Tom Barker wheeled and stared at him until he turned away.

The grocer stood, the softness of his face reflecting his inner thoughts as putty reflects the ideas of the molder. "That's the question, you know," he said. "Not what we think separately. I don't like science no more than you. And the closer it comes to me and my children the less I like it. Or free love. I'm a God-fearin' man. But I don't know: Is this the Will of God expressed, or just one girl's bad dreams? After all, the Book does say, 'Thou shalt not kill.'"

"Come off it, Sak," a voice called. "We ain't talkin' 'bout killin' no one. Just shake 'em up a bit and show 'em where it's at."

"That's where it starts," agreed the grocer, "but . . ." He shook his head, then shrugged and sat back down.

Irad rose and stood, still as fate, until the noise died down and disappeared, the last eye focused on him, and the last breath was held.

"This girl," Irad said, moving his head from side to side like a hawk seeking his prey, "she either had a dream or a vision. The Lord either spoke to her or He didn't. To find out, we cannot rely on our own thinking or someone else's opinion. We must ask the Lord."

He paused and the men all looked up, as though expecting the roof to open and God's angel to appear with flaming sword in hand.

"I have asked the Lord," Irad intoned, "and He has answered

me." He stopped, waiting for a second to see if anyone dared question this. No one dared.

"This morning I went to the Book, which is the Revealed Word of the Lord, and He directed my hand to the Book of Genesis; chapter nineteen, verses twenty-four and twenty-five. Let us read them together."

Irad opened his Book and waited while a scattering of Bibles appeared and were shared and the page was found. They read:

24. *Then the* LORD *rained upon Sodom and Go-mor-rah brimstone and fire from the* LORD *out of heaven;*
25. *And he overthrew those cities, and all the plain, and all the inhabitants of the cities, and that which grew upon the ground.*

"Now I think that's pretty clear," Irad said.

~~~~~~~~~~

Peter shifted all his weight onto his right foot and concentrated earnestly on the peeling white paint covering the far wall. His right big toe was itching with the fierce intensity of the unscratch-able. Actually, he supposed he *could* scratch it, but it would look immature: bending over to scratch his toe while standing before the Table. He should have accepted their suggestion that he sit down, but it was too late now. Talking to an adult always made him feel nervous and insecure, even though now, at seventeen, he was supposed to be one himself. Talking to adults en masse was nerve-wracking. Facing the Table was sheer torture.

I do not love thee, Doctor Fell

He was going to start to giggle any second. That would rip it good! Here he was asking to take on adult responsibility, and the best he could do was stare at the conference room's peeling paint and shift from foot to foot. And itch. And think of stupid poetry.

Why this should be, I cannot tell

Sure as hell he was going to break out and giggle any second. Why couldn't he have sat down when they asked him? The thing to do was concentrate on something else. If he'd made five copies of his request then they'd all be reading it at once instead of pass-ing it down the line, giving the Table plenty of time to stare at him while it was being read. He'd remember to make five copies the next time. And to sit down. If he was lucky, maybe he'd never have to go before the Table again. No more requests, that was the answer. And tread the narrow path so he'd never get called up. And scratch his foot.

But this I know, and know full well

Shit! If he couldn't even control his own mind . . .

"Peter Thrumager."

"Huh? I mean, yes?" Peter suddenly had no desire to giggle. Joseph leLane, Ph.D., recognized head of Palisades Enclave even when he wasn't taking his turn as chairman of the Table of Deans, leaned heavily on the table in front of him: "We have read your request and will now begin formal discussion.

"To start it off: You have a nicely thought-out statement here, including a well-worded paragraph on the importance of the, ah, step you propose taking. Do you feel that you really understand the meaning—the import—of the words you've laid out here?"

Peter's mind whirled around, but nothing came to the top. "Excuse me?" he asked.

LeLane sighed. "Sit down, Peter. Pull that chair over."

Peter gratefully dragged the wooden chair over in front of the table, sat down, and crossed his legs, bringing his foot into scratching range.

"Now," leLane continued, "you want to get married?"

Peter nodded. That's what the request said.

"Why?"

"Well, sir—" All of a sudden Peter couldn't figure out what to do with his hands. He clenched his fists and crossed his arms over his chest. "I explained in the request."

"That's so," leLane agreed. "Please explain again. In your own words. Mind you, Peter, there's nothing wrong with copping the language of your request from library copies of earlier requests. Nothing at all. One is not required to be an original thinker to get married; only to get a doctorate. Even then, ah—never mind. However, we would like to know if you understand fully what you're requesting.

"What is the function of marriage within the enclave?"

"Well . . ." Peter thought quickly. "Well" is a useful word for gaining enough time to start your brain turning over. "Well, as opposed to the traditional meaning of marriage, as still practiced outside the enclaves for example, which is a religious ritual to formalize social and sexual taboos; marriage here in the enclave, and in the other, ah, what Dr. leLane has called 'enclaves of sanity,' is a declaration of intent to have children and a compact of agreement to raise, educate, and care for them."

LeLane nodded. The other three Table members were content with merely staring at Peter. "You're basically right," leLane said, "except for your assumption that the other enclaves are so much like ours. They progress in their own ways, like the rest of what's left of society. But if marriage is merely a declaration of intent in Palisades Enclave, why do you have to make a request before the Table?"

"I—I never thought about it."

"That's honest," leLane admitted, "but it's not good enough."

"As a matter of fact," Mrs. Tomlin said from her left-corner position at the table, "you've got it just about exactly reversed. That is, your facts are right, but your causes are reversed." Her voice seemed too husky for her slight frame. "In the village they gave up birth control along with the rest of 'science.' 'Science' is their catch-all phrase for everything they're afraid of, everything they disapprove of, and everything they can't make work anymore. That's why they went back to the old forms of marriage. It makes sense. If a woman is liable to get pregnant any time she screws, in a society where momma has to stay home and take care of the kids all day, there'd better be a poppa. By the same token, if poppa is going to be responsible for any kids momma produces, he probably wants to be reasonably sure they're his kids."

LeLane pushed his palms against the table. "It makes sense, of course it does. And their fear of us and our 'science' makes sense. It's our attitude toward them that doesn't. It's a good idea to make sure the lion is well fed before you enter the cage, but it makes more sense to stay out of the cage entirely."

"I agree," Mrs. Tomlin said. "Entirely, I agree. But if you *must* enter the cage, the least you can do is try to feed the lion."

"Fine," leLane growled. "But one of these days we're going to get an arm chewed off!"

Peter felt completely lost in the conversation. It was, he realized, the continuation of an old argument and had little to do with him.

"Why?" leLane continued. "We supply their government for them, their laws for them, their medicine for them; and if anyone in that town down there ever finds out that the traveling judge or the circuit doctor comes from the enclave, and not from the Duchy, they'd riot—at least. They think we're immoral and evil."

"And you?" Mrs. Tomlin asked. "You think *they're* narrow-minded, bigoted, and stupid."

"Right!"

"And their kids grow up knowing only that way of life and be-lieving in it—except to the extent that we show them there *is* something different. And in a few score years we're right back where we were before the Death killed off ninety per cent of hu-manity: bigoted little villages growing into provincial little states and chauvinistic countries all set to blow each other back into bigoted little bits. Blah. We *must* try to help them—to counter-balance their retreat into ignorance—if not for them, then for their children; if not for their children, then for ours."

LeLane shook his head from side to side, further disturbing the cloud of white hair. "I can't say you're wrong," he said. "But some-times I feel like—have you ever heard of narapoia?"

Peter started: the question had been addressed to him. "No, sir," he replied.

"It's the opposite of paranoia," leLane told him. "It's the delu-sion that you're following someone else around, with the secret intention of doing him good."

"Yes, sir," Peter said.

"A sense of humor wouldn't hurt you, son," leLane said se-verely. "Oh, hell—where were we?"

"Ah . . ." Peter said.

"Marriage here in the enclave—within our little tribe, if you like," Mrs. Tomlin picked up, "serves an entirely different pur-pose. But it *is* important. Just as important—no, more important —than down in the town. It's a declaration of reasoned intent on the part of both the man and the woman." She wasn't speaking obliquely to leLane anymore, Peter saw, but directly to him.

"Yes, ma'am," he agreed.

"Why?" she demanded.

"Well . . ." There it was again. "Okay," he said, "look. What it means to me is just—we want to have a kid. So I guess in getting married we're saying that we're ready, or we think we are, to stay together and to bring up a kid."

"When, may I ask, were you planning to have this child?" le-Lane asked kindly.

"Well, sometime soon."

"I think . . . no, I'll spare you any more of our inter-Table squabbles. Your request is denied for now. The next time you ask, if it's at least six months from now, it's quite liable to be granted; so be careful."

The others nodded their agreement. Peter couldn't help wondering by what sort of telepathy they had communicated and discussed his request while he was sitting in front of them and hadn't heard a word.

"Yes, sir," he said extremely politely. "Thank you."

"I canceled my appointment," Ruth said. "It would be kind of pointless now. I'm sorry, Peter."

Peter looked at the slim, dark girl standing in front of him: six inches shorter than he, fifty pounds lighter, four months younger, and, in some ways, infinitely more mature. "Me too," he said. "I'm sorry. You could go ahead with it, you know. I'm sure they'd okay your request."

"Then what?" Ruth asked, smiling gently up at him. "You're supposed to have your partner in mind when you request a marriage, not get a clearance and then shop around. And I do have a partner in mind—very much in mind." She sat down on the bench next to him and put her hand over his.

Peter shrugged. "Thank you. I mean, I love you too; but if you wait for me, you're going to be an old maid with a lover."

"Six months," Ruth said.

"Maybe."

Ruth pushed out her lips in a thoughtful pout. "You know, I don't really think I'd mind waiting another couple of years to have a baby. I took care of my kid sister for almost a year when my mother went to take that special course in narco-something-or-other at the hospital in Diego Enclave. In some ways it's pretty much of a drag."

Peter stood up and took her hand. "Come," he said. "Walk."

They walked slowly down the path that twisted away behind the classrooms, each suddenly shy in the presence of the other.

"This way," Ruth said, pulling ahead of him. "Remember?"

"I remember," Peter answered, following her along the narrow trail that they had first walked eight months before. "It's over-grown."

"Our special place," Ruth said. "Where we can be alone to just stare at each other. Or to make love. Or to talk and plan." She quoted: " 'The need for time to plan and do . . .' "

Peter stopped, put his arms around Ruth, and pulled her to him. "You remember?"

"Of course I remember," she murmured into his lips. "You wrote it for me."

"It's childish," Peter insisted as they walked arm in arm deeper into the wood.

"It's not! I'd remember it anyway, even if it were, but it's not!"

We will number this year one

She stopped to kiss him under the friendly stoop of a willow.

And count off time and tide from here.

"Don't recite it."

"I want to. I love you."

The need for time has just begun
And can but grow from year to year:

"A year longer than we thought."

"We'll have enough years. I love you."

Again they kissed. He pulled her down onto the soft, damp grass under the willow and they lay together, groping for each other under the impediment of summer clothing.

The need for time to plan and do
In brief-flown days from sun to sun;
The years are short, and all too few,
But we will number this year one.

They moved together.

~~~~~~~~~~

3

Mordecai Lehrer rode slowly into town. His wagon was heavily loaded and his mule was old. Already, on the edge of town, he had picked up an entourage: a group of solemn-faced children paced slowly beside the wagon, holding on to one or another of the leather straps that bound up the side panels, cautiously petting the slow-moving black beast on its matted flank, or just staring wide-eyed and open-mouthed at the strange-looking, tall old man with the floppy black hat, worn gray robes, and snow-white beard.

Except for the children, the town seemed deserted. Usually, as he rode through the dusty street, women would come to their door or peer through their windows to watch the passage of the peddler and mentally list the pins, needles, pots, pans, spools of thread, balls of yarn, and bolts of fabric they would need from him before he left town. Usually by now one of the men, at his wife's insistence, would have come up to the wagon and invited him to dinner, so that the good woman could hear the latest gossip from the duke's court in San Francisco, forty miles to the north.

This day was not usual, and Mordecai worried about the unusual. "Boy!" he called to the youth who was practicing walking backward by the side of the mule. "Intelligent-looking lad. Where are your elders this morning? Where are your parents?"

"Meetin' hall," the youth replied briefly.

"Ah! Of course. Bright lad! Town meeting today?"

"Trial."

Mordecai nodded, causing his beard to flap. "Good lad. Be brief. Loquaciousness is always suspect in any society whose members have mislaid their sense of humor. It is, unfortunately, this very sense of humor and not the opposable digit that marks Man from the brute. I am very much afraid that we move quickly toward brutality, my taciturn friend. But I talk too much, forgive me. I am an old man, and that is a privilege of the old." He leaned far forward and fixed the boy with his intent, blue eyes. "What . . . sort . . . of . . . trial?" he asked, giving each word its full weight.

"Witchcraft."

"Witch—"

And the spigot opened: "Witchcraft! They's got two witches in there. They caught 'em somewheres up by the enclave doin' witchin'-type thin's and brought 'em back. My dad says it's time us decent, God-fearin' folk put the fear of God into them weirds up in the 'clave. They went up to see what them weirds was plottin' up there—on account of Mrs. Siddens' vision—and they caught these two funny-catin' against the Word of God and they's brought 'em down and they's settin' 'em on trial and everyone's in there watchin' and my ma put on her Sunday dress and all and they won't even let us kids in and them two witches don't hardly look growed up themselves and I don't think it's fair!" And he paused for breath and then realized how many words he'd said all at once, and the breath caught in his throat and he flushed red to the tips of his ears.

"Witchcraft!" Mordecai rumbled from somewhere deep in his chest, sitting stock upright and glaring across at the meeting hall. "You're right, my discerning young friend, I don't think it's fair either." He clicked twice, sharply, and his mule walked promptly over to the nearest post and stopped. "Watch my wagon for me, young sir, and I will take advantage of my advanced years to go where children are not permitted."

Mordecai strode across the hot, dusty square, snatched off his hat, and stomped up the wooden steps of the meeting hall. The one-room interior of the frame building was so crowded that it seemed to bulge outward slightly at the four walls, and the back of the hall was so packed that Mordecai went unnoticed as he wedged himself among the standing-room-only crowd. His height enabled him to get a good view of the room over the heads of the ear-to-ear and chin-to-shoulder devotees of courtroom drama who breathed and sweated hotly and silently, mouths open and noses pointed sharply toward the front of the room.

The brightness of the forenoon sun reflected off the fine, white streetdust and came in through the parallel rows of blindless windows, which gaped open in hopes of inducing a breeze. This produced a sort of garish light without shadows that bleached out color and kindness, texture and reality, and turned the scene into a stylized center panel of some hellish triptych; a *Grand Guignol* parody of a trial.

The dumb and motionless townspeople who made up the audience would not dare cough to break the hushed silence, but their breathing filled the room. A waist-high railing separated the actors from the audience. It was flanked by a pair of ancient, filthy flags and broken at the aisle by a canted, swinging gate with a high-pitched creak that snapped like a pistol shot.

Center stage was a long table, behind which sat, smug and stern, the leaders of the town. Stage right and left held smaller tables for defense and prosecution. And far left, in a double row of chairs, frozen into attitudes of uncomfortable concentration: the jury.

A witness stood, clutching the back of a chair, between the main table and the jury. He was young and ill at ease. Although he kept his face rigidly forward, his gaze darted around the room. He fought, and thus worsened, a tendency to stammer, and his knuckles were white from his grip on the wood slab chairback.

A tall, thin man in black paced slowly back and forth before the jury, his body leaning at an unnatural angle, and led the witness. His was the only motion in the room, and the steady, hypnotic *thud* of his step slowly weighed down the soul.

"You saw? Come, come, my friend, you may not stop there. You must tell the group, the assemblage, the jury, and your God just what you saw, and thus purge yourself of associative sin. You must purge yourself. You saw?"

"I . . . well, I saw them there, those two, the defendants, at that table there. I saw them. I *saw* them." Almost wonderingly.

"Yes, you did. Of course you did. What did they do? What did you see?"

The breathing stopped.

"I saw . . . well, they was layin'-like together under this tree. I mean, well, we was already there, like hidin' there when they came down, walkin' and touchin'—I mean like they was already *touchin'* when they walked down. We stayed hidden, see, 'cause we hadn't like decided what to, ah, how to, ah—wh, uh, were just kind of in the underbrush there and we kept quiet. They was twelve of us—"

"I know."

"Well, you said to say it like you wasn't there, so I—"

"You're right, friend Lang, and I apologize. Continue."

"Well, they stopped by this tree, see, and then they kind of sat down, and then they was layin' down. Their hands was all over each other."

"Was there any conversation?"

"Not then. Like I said, we was hidin'—"

"Yes, but did *they* talk to each other?"

"Oh. Yes they did." He looked around and nodded his head quickly up and down.

"How far were you from the defendants?"

"I guess I was the closest. Yes, I was. Of our group, you know. I was, maybe, eight-ten yards away, layin' down."

"Could you hear them clearly?"

"Yes. Yes, sir, I could."

"What were they saying?"

"Well, they was kind of talkin' about, you know, lovin' each other, and then they was kissin', and then she—the girl—like recited somethin' and that's when they was layin' down and they come to each other and they was pettin' each other and their clothes was kind of half off and they was—they was—they was fornicatin'."

He paused and rolled the word around in his mouth and then spat it out again: "*Fornicatin'!*"

Had someone a pin to perform the time-honored experiment, it would have sounded like a cannon shot as it hit the floor.

Mordecai felt a coldness wad itself up into a tight ball in his stomach. He looked at Irad, who dominated the room like a great, black bird, and thought of similes and lined them up neatly for inspection: Torquemada at prayer; Pontius Pilate stooped over a basin of water; Titus Oates smiling.

The two accused were sitting, silent and bewildered, at the far table. The boy Mordecai recognized from the enclave, but he didn't know his name. The girl was Ruth, daughter of one of the enclave's two doctors. *Fornicating!* Witchery indeed!

Irad turned and swooped back to the witness. "You say the girl recited something?"

"She did. I heard her. A sort of rhyme or poem or some such."

"Could it have been," Irad paused and looked significantly at the jury, "a *spell?*"

There was a great intake of breath.

The witness considered, recollected, analyzed, made judgment, and decided. "It could," he stated. "I'm not in the way of bein' too familiar with spells, but it *were* a rhyme, and it didn't sound like no poetry I ever heard."

"So. And this spell, this witchery, came right before what action?"

The audience leaned forward.

"They was, you know, they was kissin' and all. And she said this spell and he kissed her a great bit and rolled on top of her and they was, you know, they was doin' it. Fornicatin'. They was. And then you came out from behind the bush and stopped them and made them get decent and told them about what it says in the Bible and we took them back here."

"So! I thank you very much, friend Lang, and the Lord thanks you, for you do His work. You may step down now."

Irad hunched forward and glared around while Lang disappeared back into the crush. He was inspecting faces, peering into the eyes of the jurors, counting the intent noses of the spectators. After a long pause he raised one finger to the sky. "They don't read the Bible! They have ignored the Word! They live in sin! Sin! They are idolators. They would preserve the ways that brought the wrath of the Lord over the entire Earth in recent days."

His audience listened closely, not needing to be told who "they" were. A few of them unconsciously ran their tongues over their dry lips.

"Is it any wonder," Irad asked, swinging his finger from side to side to accent the meter of his phrases, "is it a surprise, can any of us doubt, can there be any question as to what this means? Have we here then a simple case of fornication? Would not that be sin enough; fornication? No!

"It's witchcraft! Witch-doing, witch-planning, witch-scheming, pact-with-the-devil, sure-as-sin witchcraft! There is no doubt in my mind. Do any of you doubt? Did you not hear of spells and such? That's what they teach 'em in that place: witchery!

"And we know what the Book says about witches."

Irad went on, but Mordecai backed away and out the door. He slowly and firmly settled his hat back over his white hair and walked down the steps and across the square to his wagon.

"Did you see 'em?" the boy demanded. "Did you see the witches?"

"I didn't see any witches," Mordecai told him. "I saw two frightened children and a mob, but no witches. Only special people can see witches, and they will see them regardless."

"Regardless?" the boy asked, wondering.

Mordecai excavated a well-wrapped square of chocolate from its resting place in the depths of the wagon and solemnly handed it to the lad. "Regardless of anything we do," he replied.

"Oh?"

Mordecai nodded his head. "Oh!" He climbed up to his seat and clicked at the mule. Beast, wagon, and peddler clopped across the square.

The mule came to rest on a side street, and Mordecai sat there for over an hour, chin resting on breastbone, thinking circular thoughts. The meeting hall emptied then, and a cluster of people came by, murmuring the news. Mordecai listened closely. He sighed when they had passed, and lifted his head. Raising his eyes to a cloudy heaven, he softly chanted a prayer in a language as old as the Bible.

It was midnight when the door to the small jail opened. The two jailors looked up to see the old peddler framed by the night.

"Yes, old man?" the senior asked. "What can we do for you?"

"I saw the light," Mordecai said. "You're up late."

"All night, old man."

"To pass the time," Mordecai suggested, pulling a glossy, new pack of cards from his coat. "Merely for entertainment, you understand."

The jailors eyed the cards. "You have no place to sleep tonight?" the younger inquired.

Mordecai shrugged. "An old man doesn't require much sleep anyhow."

They played rummy. Mordecai showed them a three-handed version, and they played it for over an hour. No wagering, of course, although they did keep track of points. No mention was made of the two prisoners in the cells behind the closed door.

Mordecai spoke of thirst. The jailors reflected on thirst, thought long about thirst, and made thirst a part of them. Mordecai spoke of cider, which he carried in his wagon.

The jug was heavy and the cider was cool. The jailors produced two mugs and a glass, which Mordecai filled, and they gulped the first filling quickly down and the mugs were refilled. Mordecai sipped at his glass.

The jailors found themselves getting hot and drowsy. The senior loosened his shirt and fumbled with the seven cards in his hand. He couldn't seem to read them. He looked across at his junior, who had dropped his cards and was leaning, slumped down, across the arm of his chair. *That's no help,* the senior thought fuzzily as he slid into a light, red haze.

Mordecai examined the two men. They were breathing in deep syncopation, and their focus of attention had turned inward. He lifted them to the floor and arranged them side by side under the corner table.

The jail's keys, on the traditional great ring, were in the top drawer of an old metal desk that was slowly rusting out at the back of the office. Mordecai sorted the keys and unlocked the door that led to the cells. Lighting a kerosene lantern, he held it before him and walked down the cell corridor.

The boy and girl, who were the jail's only guests, were in opposite cells, separated by the corridor. The boy was asleep on his small cot, and the girl sitting on the edge of hers, staring into the night. She didn't seem to be aware of Mordecai's presence, nor of the light, nor of the passage of time. Mordecai opened the door of her cell and she didn't notice. He passed the lantern in front of her eyes, and they refused to track.

Peter had awakened to the noise and light. He sat up and glared at Mordecai. "Who are you? What do you want? It isn't morning yet."

"At least you can see me," Mordecai commented. "Now I know what it is to be a ghost. How long has she been like this?"

"Why don't you leave her alone?" Peter demanded. "Why don't all of you leave her alone?"

"I'm all of me there is," Mordecai said, going over to Peter's cell and unlocking it. "Could I, perhaps, interest you in departing from this hostelry before the landlord comes to collect the rent?"

"What?" Peter asked, coming over to the open door of his cell and squinting out at Mordecai.

"Do you want to get out of here?"

"Of course I— Aren't you the peddler? The one that comes around every six months or so?"

"Mordecai himself, in the somewhat weary flesh."

"Thank God. Then you're not one of them. Do you know what they were planning to do to us? They're going to hang Ruth. *Hang* her. At noon. Because she's a witch. A witch! I still don't believe— What the hell are you doing?"

While Peter spoke, Mordecai had gone back into Ruth's cell and knelt down facing her. Suddenly he slapped her across the face. The sharp sound echoed off the cement walls, and Ruth gasped, her eyes wide, and jerked convulsively. Peter leaped toward Mordecai, but before he could traverse the two cells Ruth shuddered and buried her face in Mordecai's coat, and was sobbing softly while Mordecai patted her hair. "That's all right," he insisted firmly. "You're all right now. We're going to get you out of here, and you'll be fine. It's almost over. Just take it easy and listen to me and you'll be home soon."

Peter stopped in front of Mordecai, his arms waving uselessly about. He pulled them to his side and stared down at the two of them. "I guess you know what you're doing," he said. "I wish I knew what I was doing, or what I'd done. Why do these people hate us like that? They want to hang Ruth because she's a witch, and they're not sure whether I'm a witch or not so they're going to press me with great stones until they find out. What does that mean, 'press me with great stones'?"

"I saw a picture once, in a book," Mordecai said without looking up. "You wouldn't like it." He helped Ruth to her feet, and

produced a large handkerchief from some inner pocket for her
to wipe her face. "How do you feel?" he asked.

"Miserable," Ruth said, forcing the words out through layers
of shock and hurt, from some core of sanity deep inside. "The
way they looked at me . . . The things they said . . ."

"You must get out of here," Mordecai said. "Now. Don't even
try to talk any more. Son, you help me."

The two of them helped Ruth down the short corridor to the
front room, Peter submerging his fright in his concern for Ruth.
By the end of the corridor Ruth's head had re-established control
over her legs and she was able to walk. Only her unnaturally wide
eyes and tentative movements showed how tight that control was.

Ruth sat in a wooden chair by the desk, her fingers digging into
its arms and her eyes ceaselessly darting from left to right like a
frightened deer's. Peter spotted the two pairs of boots sticking
out from under the table and squatted down to look. His courage, squashed out of him by the trial, was slowly welling back.
"What happened to them?" he asked.

"They are in a better world," Mordecai said firmly.

"Are they—are they dead?" Ruth asked, twisting around to look
against her will.

"As tourists only," Mordecai assured her. "They are asleep.
They'll sleep for quite a while yet, and they might have a slight
headache when they awake, but nothing worse. You two hardened
sinners will please remain quiet and humble while I investigate
the outside world."

"Hardened—" Peter said in a burst of air.

"Merely an old man's wry humor. A comment about this, the
best of all possible worlds. Quiet now—and keep your heads in!"
Mordecai opened the door and walked into the night with his
usual gait, his shoulders perhaps a bit less stooped. The only
thing remarkable to any outside observer was the speed and care
with which he closed the door behind him.

The wagon was waiting where he had left it by the side of the
building. His mule looked at him reproachfully for being so many
hours in harness, but made no comment. He stroked it about the
top of the head and ears for a minute, whispering those things
that a man might whisper to an old and patient friend, then led
the wagon around to the door.

He had given his eyes time to become accustomed to the moonlight and had detected no interest in the jail or himself, but there was still a nagging doubt in his mind.

Suddenly, as he reached the door, he gasped and clutched at his chest with both hands. Staggering several steps in front of the mule, he stood weaving, then closed in on himself and crumpled to the ground. Once he tried to rise before collapsing in an untidy heap on the packed earth. He lay still.

After several minutes the mule pulled his load slowly forward and nuzzled the motionless body. Shortly the beast became concerned and poked more sharply at his master, making soft, worried coughs deep in his throat.

Mordecai reached for the animal's harness and pulled himself up. He wrapped his arms around the mule's neck and held it firmly for a long moment, then went back to the wagon and undid several leather straps, released two obscure catches, took a garment from a deep drawer, and removed a small package from a subtly placed niche.

"I hope I haven't been unduly long," he said, carefully shutting the door behind him.

"Not more than a year or two," Peter replied. "I could have sworn I saw the dawn three times while you were gone."

"Accept my humblest apologies," Mordecai said. "I know how it feels. I shan't, I sincerely hope, do it again. Now then, to the problem at hand." He undid the garment, deftly removing several straight pins and bits of string. "A wool checked shirt, the largest size I have in stock. Not so impressive when you reflect that I only have three sizes: small, medium, and large. The bottom, I fear, has dropped out of the ready-to-wear market." He displayed it, front and back. "The latest in outergarments for milady's spring wardrobe. Normally three Washington dollars or the equivalent in local currency or barter. But not for you, my dear; a special price for you. Free. And you can pay later."

Ruth took the shirt and clutched it to her. "Thank you," she said dully. "I'm not cold."

"You will be. You're going to ride out of this charming metropolis on my first-class accommodation. Unfortunately, it is also my third-class accommodation. I call it the hidey-hole. Picturesque, *nu?* It's kind of cramped, and the heating isn't too good. Put the shirt on."

Ruth enveloped herself in the large man's shirt and buttoned it up the front.

"*Nu?*" Peter repeated.

"An ancient and honorable Yiddish expression," Mordecai told him. "It means: 'so what else?' "

"Yiddish," Peter repeated, as though fixing the word in his mind.

Mordecai sighed. "Youth! It always has trouble believing that anything in the world is older than it is. Now to the other half of the problem: you."

Ruth suddenly looked frightened. "Peter?"

"So?" Mordecai extended his hand. "Mordecai. A pleasure, Peter. Now," he rubbed his hands together thoughtfully, "unfortunately my hidey-hole isn't large enough for two, no matter how friendly they are. Don't glare at me; I have a dirty mind, but I enjoy it, and my concept of evil is highly refined. *Honi soit qui mal y pense;* and ask someone else to explain it, we're in something of a hurry." While he spoke he was unwrapping the package.

"I'll stay behind," Peter said, standing up gingerly, "if you can get Ruth away from here. I can hide somewhere in town and sneak away tomorrow night."

"Nice of you to offer," Mordecai said kindly, "but I'm afraid it won't work. When they find you gone, they'll search this town so thoroughly it'll be free of cockroaches for a month. I have a better notion." He pulled the last of the wrappings off the package and displayed the contents.

"What is that?" Ruth asked. "It looks like a mess of white hair."

"Indeed," Mordecai agreed, lifting the object and shaking it out. "In the shape, you will observe, of a beard."

"Oh," Peter said. He dropped down into the chair he was poised in front of. "You mean you want me—"

"You will become me. An innocent masquerade. I have a fondness for masquerades. I will become, in turn, a guardian of law and order. Someone, after all, must watch the premises while our two friends sleep it off. An evil might be perpetrated; a sin might be, ah, enacted; a crime might be committed; a cell might be burgled; it is an awesome responsibility, but I will bear up. This little bottle contains spirit gum with which to affix your beard. A breath of alcohol will remove it at the other end of your journey. Here, allow me." He plastered Peter's chin and jowls with spirit gum and then carefully pressed the beard into place.

"There!" He stood back and critically examined his work. "Your own mother . . . my own mother . . . one second!" He reached into one of the inside pockets of his coat and pulled out a pair of scissors. "A little off the sides, a touch at the edge—*voilà!* Sorry, my manicurist has run off with a rich Armenian. You'll do, you'll pass. At a distance, of course, but that's all we can hope for. I have neither the provisions nor the skill for wrinkles. I'll study up, and next time—wrinkles, of course! Excuse me a second."

"But you'll be here when they come for us in the morning," Peter said, watching Mordecai bend over the pot-belly stove and extract soot from its innards.

"I shall," Mordecai agreed, placing himself in front of Peter and pulling a toothbrush from his breast pocket. "But you won't, and that's the important thing. Witchcraft indeed!" He dipped the toothbrush into the soot and applied fine lines to Peter's face. "Wrinkle your forehead. No, the other way—scrunch up your eyebrows."

"But what will you say to them?"

"I'll think of something."

Ruth reached over and took the old man's hand. "Thank you, Mordecai," she said. "You—you're beautiful!"

"Nonsense," Mordecai said, absently patting her hand while he admired his work. "I'm human, is what. Sometimes you must do something to affirm that fact. Sometimes you're called upon to pay the debt. Sometimes . . ." He looked down at her. "Never mind that. Live a good and happy life, my child. And I call you that only from the secure plateau of advanced age. Grow strong and wise as you grow old. Be firm in your beliefs, and don't be afraid to do what you know is right, even in the face of general disapproval—which is harder to take than physical pain. Which, at times, may encompass physical pain. And remember to tell your mother that the instruments she wanted are in the top, right, front drawer of the wagon. The box of vials labeled *Penicillium argii* contains a surprisingly adequate antibiotic variant. One to a customer for most infections."

"I'll remember," Ruth promised.

"Right. Now, ah, the hat!" He removed the ancient, broad-brimmed black felt from his own head and settled it firmly over Peter's, where it fell over the eyes. "Hm. That won't do. Ah, some wadding, of course." He took a well-worn shirt from a peg on the wall and ripped a strip from the back, which he folded and inserted around the inside of the brim. When he tried it again, it pulled down to just above Peter's eyes without quite covering them. "T'will do, t'will suffice," Mordecai grumbled, and unbuttoned his coat. "The final step in the transformation. Button it up all the way. Watch the beard! That's it. Perfect. For this limited need, anyway. What are you two staring at? Something wrong with my shirt? I have, maybe, a hole in my pants?"

"No, sir," Ruth said quickly.

"What," Peter asked respectfully, "are those?"

"These? Ah! Suspenders. Relics of the past, though farmers are starting to use them again. They hold your pants up. Come along, let's get you two out of here. You know the road? Just give the mule his head and let him set the pace. It'll seem frighteningly slow, but you'll be well gone from here by dawn and should be back to the enclave before they miss you. Tell Joe leLane what happened as soon as you arrive. He'll know what to do."

"Why don't you just come with us?" Peter asked. "It's so late everyone must be asleep. I could crouch down or something."

"Couldn't take the chance," Mordecai said. "I thought of that, believe me. On this night, with this day coming up, few will sleep soundly. People will be at their windows when they hear you pass. I doubt if any will be out, but the houses are close enough to the street to see an extra passenger. Particularly now, two days after full moon. If any *are* out they'll grunt a greeting as you pass. Grunt back, they will expect no more. Now . . ." He opened the door and looked out. The wagon was where he had placed it, blocking a direct view of the door from the street, and all was still.

Mordecai took two quick steps to the wagon and pulled at a strap. A section of the side, drawers and all, swung open to reveal a cubbyhole smaller than three feet in every dimension. "Come!" he whispered to Ruth. "I'll help you in. It's not spacious, but you'll have more room than you think. Here, take a pillow, it will help." He lifted her into the space, handed her a skinny cushion, stood aside while Peter stretched his head in and kissed Ruth for the first time in too frighteningly long, and swung the panel closed. "Here," he said to Peter, "watch me secure it so you know how to undo the process." He secured the two hidden catches and tightened the straps.

"What now?" Peter asked. He was shivering.

Mordecai put his arm around the youth and walked him the two steps to the front of the wagon. "It's a breeze," he said. *And now, Daniel, there's this den.* . . . "Just climb up. Click twice— you know, between your teeth—or snap the reins and he'll start up. Turn right at the corner and keep going until you run out of road. Click twice again, or pull up on the reins, and he'll stop. Good luck, Peter. *Sholom Aleichem.*"

"I'll tell Dr. leLane as soon as I get back," Peter said, fighting some emotion in his voice.

"Yes, of course you will. Get up there now!"

The boy climbed up to his seat. *He's too ginger,* Mordecai thought. *I should have told him to move slowly. The old move slowly.*

It was several hours after dawn when the first citizen rushed through the door. A small, eager man with a sagging mustache, he was well into the room before he realized that a cog of his reality was out of place.

Mordecai was settled comfortably before the desk, his sleeves rolled up, playing solitaire. It was something over his hundredth game—he had stopped counting at a hundred—and the fourteenth variety. It was losing its fascination.

The two regulars were still resting comfortably under the table, although the younger was showing signs of motion.

The small man spotted the boots after staring curiously at Mordecai for something over a minute. "What happened?" he demanded, pacing forward and bobbing his head back and forth like a mustached quail.

"Where?" Mordecai asked curiously.

The man ceased all motion and stared at Mordecai. Then he swiveled and stared under the table. Then he darted across the room and flung open the door to the cells. Again he stared. Then he pranced back across the room and stopped in front of Mordecai. "What happened to *them?*" He pointed. "Where are *they?*" Again he pointed. "And what are you doing here?" He didn't point this time, contenting himself with glowering.

"Solitaire," Mordecai explained. "Klondike, it's called. I need a red jack."

The man's mustache bristled, and he backed slowly through the outer door. Then he slammed it and raced off down the street.

Three more hands, Mordecai predicted to himself. He was somewhat proud to find himself outwardly calm. Not completely, and he was glad of that too, in an obscure way. He gathered the cards and reshuffled.

He was on his fourth hand when the crowd appeared at the door, but one game had been unnaturally short.

Four men detached themselves from the crowd and entered the room, carefully ignoring Mordecai. One of them went to inspect the prone jailers, and the other three strode to the cells.

"Breathin'," the one announced.

"Gone!" one of the three declared. They all turned to stare at Mordecai, but none of them made a move. The room grew still.

"Peddler!" a deep voice projected from the doorway.

Mordecai gently put down his cards and swiveled around.

Irad stood just inside the door, tall and thin and enjoying a righteous wrath. "You were seen leaving town during the night."

"They must have been mistaken," Mordecai said softly.

"Mistaken!" Irad growled. "Your wagon left town, but we can assume it held a different crew."

"You may assume what you like."

Irad grew even taller. "You have knowingly aided evil, and therefore you are evil! Mordecai the peddler, you know me?"

Mordecai nodded slowly. "I know you, Irad, grandson of Cain."

Irad blanched. "What? You . . ."

"As you might expect," Mordecai said, "I am something of a biblical scholar. Old Testament only, I assure you. Curious, the history of your name. Your parents—"

"Peddler!" Irad roared. "If you study the Bible, whatever your purpose, you must know its injunction: 'an eye for an eye.'

"You have allowed, nay—abetted, two malefactors to escape justice. Therefore you must suffer as they, in their place. That is our judgment. Have you anything to say, peddler?"

Mordecai shrugged. "*Nu?*" he said.

4.

~~~~~~~~

It was already almost eleven, and he was most certainly going to be late, which would never do. Dr. Norbert Enrico Pepperidge, cochairman of the Department of Physics, University of Chicago, touched the whip gently to his mare's flanks in hopes of speeding the beast up without having to apply any more persuasive measure. After all, he could understand the horse's point of view perfectly well: if *he* were the horse, pulling a two-wheeler over a cracked and overgrown stretch of ancient two-lane asphalt in the questionable illumination of a kerosene driving lamp, he'd be damned if he'd go any faster.

The mare apparently thought as Dr. Pepperidge did, for she went no faster. Pepperidge found himself torn between empathizing with the animal and beating her. He clicked his tongue and shook the reins, and the mare merely turned to look at him without pausing in her methodical gait.

"Come on, Emily, old girl," he said, wrapping his cloak more firmly about him. "A bit more interest in your job, if you will." The mare turned away, but made no effort to speed up. Pepperidge couldn't bring himself to use any more forceful measure, and he resigned himself to being late. It didn't really matter, he wasn't needed for the first few hours anyway; but it was bad for morale. It set a bad example for the undergraduates when a full professor showed any human feelings.

A thick stand of trees encroached the road, some rooting in fissures in the roadbed itself. Mostly they grew toward the edge where the asphalt was thinner and temperature change and weather could accomplish their inevitable work more quickly; but an occasional great tree thrust itself through the crown of the road, peeling the bed aside like a foil wrapper. Where several of these road-rooted trees stood close together Pepperidge had to get out of his cart and help wedge it around the corner. There were already places where a four-wheeler couldn't get through.

Along the side of the road could be made out the shells of what had been houses seventy years before. Many of them burnt out, most of them looted, all of them suffering the extreme structural damage seven decades of neglect will cause in a house that was not built to outlast the original owner. They looked strangely unreal in the dark—an endless row of artificial shapes built to appease some powerful but arcane geometer's god. Cairns of an unknown civilization whose needs and purposes can but be guessed at by modern man. Or possibly the misshapen homes of a race of grotesque beings, creatures from Earth's prehistory, long hidden from the sight of man but now returning to former haunts.

From prehistory, Pepperidge thought, to posthistory. He found the idea amusing. From prehistory to posthistory in four thousand years. And now, with the breakdown of everything that was civilization, the goblins were indeed returning; coming out of their secure hiding places in the human mind. A hundred years ago total literacy was an almost realized goal; today only those in the enclaves could read, or wanted to, and nowhere was anyone printing books. A hundred years ago scientists had penetrated to the particles within the particles of the atom, had gazed upon the stars that made up distant galaxies, and had placed men upon other worlds. Today, seventy-three years after the appearance of the Death, "science" was a curse word outside the enclaves, and mostly a memory inside. The atom was once more inviolable, the distant galaxies invisible, and the men on the other worlds were cruelly fated to remain there, barred from returning to Earth by that mutated ECHO virus known as the Death.

The trees halted in a clean straight line to the left of the carriage, giving way to a large field of concrete sparsely studded with weeds. It must have been the parking lot for the one-story brick structure barely visible in the darkness behind it. In the center of the concrete was a large, red plastic obelisk that reflected the moonlight so much better than its surroundings that it seemed almost to glow with a light of its own. Inset black letters said: C T I SEMICONDUCTORS, and barring accident would keep saying it for the next ten thousand years. Man's Golden Age mementos, objects for all of time to admire: plastic signs, glass beer bottles, and porcelain crappers. Pepperidge had an image of future, simpler generations praying and sacrificing to similar obelisks about the world, and of shamans using the mysterious graven words in their spells. "CTI Semiconductors," he murmured to his mare, "truly a name to conjure with." Emily ignored him and plodded on.

Ten minutes later Dr. Pepperidge arrived at the site. He was indeed late, but his well-drilled team had gone ahead very nicely without him. The site was a cleared field about a hundred yards square. Kerosene lamps set on posts scattered about the field gave a fluttery, inadequate light to the area, plunging the unlit portions into deep shadow without providing enough lighting to pull the rest out of gloom. The field was covered by a grid of two-foot square wooden platforms, chest-high, about ten feet apart. Each platform was topped with a square wooden frame fitted with a drumskin of aluminum foil. The frames were fastened by two wooden pegs on the east-west axis to larger frames which were fixed on the north-south axis to the platform. This made it possible to adjust each square of aluminum foil to face any direction and hold its position.

"Welcome, sir," Tobias, a tall, moon-faced senior said, taking the reins and helping Pepperidge down from the cart. "We're proceeding with the setting up, as you see, sir, without any problems. Just go on, sir; I'll have one of the freshmen take care of the rig."

"You're a good man, Tobias," Pepperidge said, wondering whether he was being flattered or condescended to. "No need to have her walked, that's all she's done; but see that she gets some water."

"Yes, sir. I'll see to it myself, sir."

"How long have you been a senior, Tobias?" Pepperidge asked.

"About four years now, sir. I'm just about ready to take the exams for journeyman."

"Very good. Are you scheduled?"

"Yes, sir. Next month. And I have you for my orals; you and Professor Steadman."

"Aha!" Pepperidge said. Not that students weren't polite normally—after all, to be thrown out of the university, and thus the enclave, was a form of ostracism that one didn't normally survive—but when a senior offers to hold your horse, and calls you "sir" twice in every sentence, it's time to look for motivation. "What are your majors?" Pepperidge asked.

"The 'dead' is X-ray crystallography," Tobias told him, "and the 'quick' is interior water systems."

Every student had to take two majors: a classical and a modern: a historical and a useful. The quick and the dead, as current slang had it.

"Thanks for warning me, Tobias," Pepperidge said. "I'll brush up on my plumbing." He nodded, hoping that Tobias would spend the next hour wondering whether he'd made a mistake, and headed across the field.

There were four hundred of the aluminum frames, set in a twenty-by-twenty array and interconnected by rays of coaxial cable emanating from the center of the field. The preparation had started early that morning, with teams of freshmen coming out to check the wooden platforms and insert the frames; making sure that the pegs were tight enough to hold securely but not too tight to allow easy positioning. Then, before dark, an assistant professor had come out with his specially trained crew to insert the squares of aluminum foil, which were held tightly in place by a turn of heavy copper wire, from which dangled the coax connectors.

The last stage of preparation, which was taking place now, was the most critical. Each of the elements—each frame—had to be lined up perpendicular to an imaginary point in the sky: the point at which the ruby pinglow of the planet Mars would be exactly fifteen minutes after the last frame was set.

Ten men, all journeyman physicists, had this job. Each carried a small, precision prism telescope with cross-hair sights and a vernier-adjusted mounting pin which slid into a slot in each of the frames. First the north-south frame was frozen onto the plane of Mars orbit. Then the east-west frame was adjusted to face where Mars would be at the proper time. Each calibration on the vernier was one degree, a distance that Mars moved across Earth's sky in four minutes.

The chief of this aiming team was an eleventh man, called the Caller, who sat in the middle of the field with his own lantern, holding in his hand a precious relic: a working stopwatch. Every four minutes he would call time and each vernier would be moved up one notch.

The call now was "ten," and final call was "fifteen," which, by simple arithmetic, gave Dr. Pepperidge twenty minutes to set up. He walked across to one of two low, windowless shacks in the east corner of the field and pushed open the door. Professor Jerob, a thin, exceptionally tall and bony, completely bald man, sat hunched over a charcoal brazier before a semicircle of lanterns. He was Pepperidge's second, and a genius in the new discipline of Resurrection: repairing century-old pieces of apparatus with the technology at hand.

"Evening, Norbert," Jerob said without looking up. "Pull up a crate and join me in prayer."

"What are we praying for?" Pepperidge asked, sitting on a bench across the brazier.

Jerob thrust a slender soldering iron back into its wire-frame holder over the coals and held up a component-heavy piece of circuit board. "This," he explained briefly.

Pepperidge took the board and held it reverently in his hands. "A workmanlike job, as usual," he commented. "What does it do?"

"It turns muscle power into electrical energy. Nine volts dc, at about one amp, to be exact. Of course, you have to hook it up to a hand-cranked generator."

"Ah?" Pepperidge said uncertainly.

"The batteries have finally given out," Jerob explained. "They won't take a charge."

"What about the spares?" Pepperidge asked.

"Them is what's given out," Jerob said. "I thought you knew. Ones we were using were tested dead last week, so we took the last off the shelf. Brand new. Well, seventy-four years old, but never been used. Pulled the plastic wrap off them, set them to charging, and about half an hour later smelled the smoke. So the preamps will have to be hand powered. And why not, I ask you? Isn't that why God created freshmen?"

Pepperidge allowed a tight smile to crease his face. "I refuse to discuss theology," he said. "Any other problems?"

"None yet. The gas generator cranked up fine when we tested it earlier. And if it'll run on what we're feeding it, it'll run on anything. No, I think if this works, we're in business."

"Well, test it out, time's getting short."

"Don't get edgy, Norbert. I still have one more connection to solder; had to wait for the iron to heat. There's plenty of time. You know I had fourteen freshmen volunteers to crank this thing? I think the image appeals to them: alone out in the middle of the field of weird cables and mirrors slowly and steadily cranking this strange apparatus to provide energy for man to listen to the planet Mars. It's like being the central character in some arcane ritual."

"You know, Jerob," Pepperidge said thoughtfully, "I wish you wouldn't use words like 'weird,' 'strange,' and 'arcane' when you talk about this. Do you really see it that way? That's damn unscientific."

"I don't see it that way," Jerob said. "I'm talking about the way these kids see it. Science *is* some sort of strange ritual to them: a cult, with them as neophyte priests. You don't think any of these kids can see the stuff we teach them as real knowledge, do you? They have to take it on faith; they don't get to see it happen. The best we can manage in the way of a lab course is a magnet picking up iron filings. We can't build them so much as a transistor, much less an integrated circuit. These kids have to take it on faith from us, and when you have to do that then it's no longer science we're dealing with. Only the stuff we can repeat today is science—the rest is magic."

"I don't see it that way," Pepperidge said. "What we're teaching these kids is true. Science is the study of the truth."

"No," Jerob objected. "Science is the study of the reproducible truth. Study of truth-because-I-say-it's-true is either religion or magic. Accept it, Norbert, you're a magician."

A youthful face peered around the edge of the door. "Frames are all set, sir," it announced.

"Very good, frosh. I'll be right out," Pepperidge said. "Okay, Jerob, I'll go crank up the receiver. Get that soldering done."

Jerob pulled the iron out of its holder and brandished it. "One minute," he stated confidently.

"That's six point six-seven per cent of the available time," Pepperidge said, "so get on the stick!" He pulled the door shut behind him before Jerob could throw the iron.

Pepperidge went around to the side of the other shack and, with an even dozen underclassmen watching expectantly, personally primed and started the generator that would provide power to the transmitters, receivers, and teleprinters inside. With only the barest preliminary protest the generator barked into life, and Pepperidge silently blessed the long-dead engineers, designers, and craftsmen who had unknowingly built for the ages. He checked the leads and connectors, the ground wire, the fuel tank, and the coaxial cable. Then he went inside the shack and checked it all from the other end. Then he turned on the master power switch and flipped the row of secondary switches: fluorescent lamps, receivers, frequency counters, signal analyzers, amplifiers, dc converters, teleprinters, digital tape recorders, paper tape punchers, paper tape readers, transmitters, and an electric coffeepot that hadn't had real coffee brewed in it for sixty years.

"All set, Norbert," Jerob said from the door, holding it open and waving toward the field. Pepperidge could see a small figure in the center of the field, hunched over a hand generator, turning it at a slow, steady rate that would deliver a steady nine volts dc to the miniature preamps where the cables came together.

"Fantastic," Pepperidge said. "Look at that!" The underclassmen had gathered beneath the lantern poles and were all standing silently with heads raised, staring at the planet Mars.

"That's mostly silent appreciation and wonder at what we are about to do," Jerob said. "But a bit of ceremony is starting to creep in. I give it ten years before it's reduced to ritual."

"You may be right," Pepperidge admitted, looking at the faces of the solemn youths. "I'm afraid that the ritual of speaking to Mars will continue long after Mars has ceased to answer. Or at least long after our equipment can no longer hear that answer. But then again perhaps it's just your pessimistic talk and the late hour that are influencing me, and everything will look better to me in the morning."

The teleprinter clattered into life, and Pepperidge dashed over to it, shouldering aside the senior hovering over the paper. "Three minutes early," he muttered. "Are we all set to transmit?"

"All ready, sir," the senior said. "The tapes are in the machine and it's set to go."

"Well, see it gets turned on at my signal, as soon as Mars signs off. This is a very short window for two-way communication."

```
RYRYRYRYRYRYRYRYRYRYRYRYRYRYRYRYRYRYRYRYRYRYRYRY
EARTH DE MARS EARTH DE MARS EARTH DE MARS EARTH DE MARS
R        Y      R        Y        R      Y      R        Y
```
THIS TWO MINUTES OF TEST TAPE IS BROUGHT TO YOU BY THE
PLANET MARS 1234567890 IS THERE INTELLIGENT LIFE ON
EARTH? MESSAGE FOLLOWS MESSAGE FOLLOWS
```
H    I    F    O    L    K    S    !    !    !    !
RYRYRYRYRYRYRYRYRYRYRYRYRYRYRYRYRYRYRYRYRYRYRYRY
EARTH DE MARS EARTH DE MARS EARTH DE MARS EARTH DE MARS
R        Y      R        Y        R      Y      R        Y
```
THIS TWO MUNUTES OF TEST TAPE IS BROUGHT TO YO
U
TEST TAPE ENDED = = MESSAGE FOLLOWS:
HELLO CHICAGO. WE HOPE YOU'RE STILL THERE AND RECEIVING.
OUR TEXT IS NINE MINUTES LONG. WE'RE GOING OVER THE LIMIT
BECAUSE THE MESSAGE IS VERY IMPORTANT. VERY IMPORTANT. WE
WILL LISTEN FOR YOUR REPLY. VERY IMPORTANT. LIFE AND DEATH.
GOOD LUCK.
TEXT:

Dr. Pepperidge read the message from Mars as it printed on the machine. Then he ripped it off and reread it while the prepared tape was being transmitted to the Ley Scientific Research Establishment, which was now a permanent colony, isolated on the airless, red surface of Mars. Then he sat down at the teleprinter and, when the tape ended, typed a careful added THANK YOU THANK YOU THANK YOU to the end of the message from Earth. Then he left the shack and walked slowly up to the crest of the bare hill behind it. On top of a hill further in the distance he could make out the skeleton of the giant dish antenna that had been set up eighty years before to talk to Ley Base, and had been burned and gutted six years before by a stray band of marauders who had presumably been angered at finding nothing of value to them amid all that scientific crap.

He sat on the cold grass with his arms wrapped around his knees and stared at the spidery structure for a long time. Then he raised his eyes to the visible stars and softly cursed them, one by one.

And then, for the first time in forty years, he cried.

~~~~~~~~~~~~~~~

5

Judge Benjamin Aristotle Crater, justice of the Fifth Circuit of the Great and Sovereign State and Independent Duchy of California, appointed by and for the People and their Hereditary Elected Representative, the governor, Duke Yammoto, drove his gig slowly, and with appropriate majesty, into town. The gig, flat black with silver trim, was a nice example of the newly reviving coachmakers' art. Judge Crater, in his severe black suit and stovepipe hat, and his two outriders in their gray suits and bowler hats, presented an image of serious, somber, intelligent, capable men engaged in important work. The outriders, on solid, sturdy horses, were the prosecuting and defense attorneys for the circuit, in which capacities they rotated.

It was a weekday morning and the men were in the fields, but word would spread and both sexes would be well represented in town by afternoon. Judge Crater did his best to put on a good show, and his court was always well filled; the majesty of the law would allow no less.

A tall man dressed in black stood on the top step of the meeting-hall entrance, awaiting the procession. His black frock coat ill fit his tall, thin body, and he moved in what seemed to be a series of small spasms rather than a continuous flow. "Judge Crater," he intoned in the full voice of the pulpit.

"Ah, yes," Judge Crater said. "Of course." He pulled his gig to a stop by the rail. "Ah. You're the, ah, you—I'm sure I remember you from the last circuit. I'm terribly sorry, but I meet so many people. I'm very bad on names."

"Irad."

"Yes?"

"My name is Irad."

"Yes. Yes, of course it is. A pleasure to see you again, Mr. Irad. Well, well; we must get down to business. Perhaps you'd be good enough to hitch my horse?" Judge Crater stepped out of his gig and started up the steps without looking back, thus leaving Irad with the choice of hitching the gig and looking servile or letting it wander and looking foolish.

The two attorneys hurried up the steps after the judge. "What did you do that for, Dr. leLane?" one of them whispered, catching up with him. "You know Irad's the power in this town."

"Right," leLane agreed. "And it's all image. I have to keep my image stronger, make him look ineffectual, foolish, and provincial. It's the little, subtle things that count. The world lost a great actor when I became a professor of psychology. And don't call me le-Lane, ever, at all, while we're here. That's all we'd need, Sandburg."

"Very good, Judge," Sandburg agreed.

"Well, let's get on with it. Can't hold up the majesty of the law. I'll settle in here and look majestic. You go around to the mayor, the justice of the peace, and the sheriff, and draw up a docket of cases. I want it presented to me by three this afternoon. And make sure that Mordecai's on it! Irad will probably try to keep him off, keep him hidden until we go away."

"Why?" Sandburg asked.

" 'I'll be the judge and I'll be the jury said cunning old fury. . . .' I imagine Irad wants to hang him without our help. Now you and Williams go get that docket made up; I'll sit here and huff." LeLane sat himself at the front table, facing the door, and took the big town ledgers out of his traveling case and opened them before him. They, he thought, added an imposing look to his solitary majesty.

A small, nervous-looking man came scurrying through the door and headed up the aisle toward the judge. His name was Barnaby something—leLane couldn't remember—and he was one of the town's four officials. There was the mayor, the JP, the sheriff, and Barnaby, who held all the other titles and did most of the work. Town clerk was the title under which he was visiting Judge Crater now; but he also served as truant officer, dog catcher, fire chief, health, building, and fire inspector, commissioner of county works, and postmaster. The titles hadn't changed in the past hundred years, but the functions of each office were drastically different. As truant officer Barnaby was responsible for runaway apprentices; dog catcher wasn't as important a job as it had been even twenty years before, when the packs of wild dogs still came out of the hills to take sheep, calves, and, it was claimed by some, an occasional child; fire chief Barnaby had the task of maintaining the great fire gong which was thumped to call out the volunteer brigade.

As health, building and fire inspector Barnaby had the responsibility for notifying the sheriff of any violation of the county codes. There were, however, no longer any written codes, and had not been in the memory of any living man. As commissioner of county works he maintained the roads—when he could get the volunteer labor force to actually go out and tar over the cracks and potholes, which was not often. As postmaster he raised the flag every morning in the town square.

As town clerk Barnaby kept all of the town records and was responsible for transferring them into the official record ledger carried by Judge Crater on his circuit.

"Mornin', Judge," Barnaby rasped, pushing through the gate in the front rail. "Should have told me you was comin'. I could have got thin's organized, saved time." Barnaby was concerned about time. He felt that he had to appear busy whenever anyone ran across him, or the town might decide that it could dispense with its clerk, dog catcher, fire chief, et cetera.

"Good morning, Barnaby," leLane said. "Good to see you again. Calm down: haste is wasteful; deliberate action looks slower but accomplishes more."

"I wish I could talk like you, Judge," Barnaby said, settling himself in front of the record book and pulling out his official notebook to copy from. "But if I don't appear hasty, why then one of these farmers is going to inquire why I don't come out and help him castrate or fence or bale, long as I got nothin' else to do, and seein' as how he's payin' my upkeep."

Barnaby uncorked his inkwell, dipped his fine-point felt-tip pen into it, and drew long lines down the flyleaf of the ledger to use up the excess ink. Then he began copying the new vital statistics into the book in the neat, square hand of the semiliterate.

The two attorneys returned to the room together, with a list of the civil and criminal actions that had been awaiting the return of Judge Crater. They handed it to Barnaby to make up the official court docket. When he finished copying the vital statistics and closed the town ledger, Barnaby would transform from town clerk to court clerk. At three o'clock he would officially hand Judge Crater the prepared docket of cases, and the session would be formally opened.

"How long is the docket?" leLane asked.

"Not bad," Williams told him. "Nine civil and five criminal cases."

"And—our friend?"

Williams nodded. "The last."

"You were right," Sandburg told him in a low voice. "They didn't want us to try him. Irad convinced the town council that Mordecai should be tried by a church court, and not a civil court."

"What church court? There aren't any."

"This one was to be made up of 'devout' townsmen, with Irad as judge. After all, he speaks with the Revealed Word of God."

"After all," leLane agreed. "How did you convince them?"

"Two telling phrases," Sandburg told him. " 'Render unto Caesar,' and when that proved weak, 'contempt of court is punishable by a fine of up to five thousand Washington dollars and a sentence of up to five years in the state penitentiary on Alcatraz Island.' "

"A masterly example of the power of rhetoric," leLane said.

The first eight cases were tried and judged between 3 P.M., when the court was called into session, and 7 P.M., when it was adjourned for the night. Good speed, even for Judge Crater, who was famous for cutting through to the pith in sharp, rapid verbal strokes. LeLane was sure, as he disrobed in the coatroom that passed for a judge's chambers, that his audience would be back tomorrow. Standing room only, he thought wryly.

They stayed overnight at the mayor's house, all three of them sharing what was probably the only guestroom in town—if you exclude the cells in the town jail. They paid for their keep with gossip about the duke's court in San Francisco; not fabricated, but imported by radio that very day.

The next morning the meeting-hall courtroom was filled and overfilled well before the arrival of Judge Crater and the start of

the court day. But somehow the audience, despite their early arrival, seemed patient rather than eager; as though they came out
of a sense of duty and not a desire to be entertained.

The remaining civil case and the first four criminal cases were
wrapped up before noon. LeLane rapped his gavel, declared a long
lunch recess, and exited the room along with his two traveling attorneys. The audience remained seated, waiting.

When court was rapped into session two hours later the spectators were still waiting. Irad had joined them and space had
been made for him in the first row. The sense of expectation had
grown until it was almost tangible. The silence was not merely
audible, it had become loud.

LeLane called the two attorneys to the bench. "Something is
going to happen," he whispered. "There is definitely some plot
or scheme in the air; I can sense it. It is for us now not to lose
our cool, as our ancestors would have put it."

"What are they planning?" Williams asked.

"I only pretend to be omniscient. Just watch yourselves and
the situation closely from now until we get out of here."

Mordecai was then brought in, and the game had begun. Sandburg and Williams flipped a coin, as custom demanded, and then
stood up to declare their prearranged positions.

"Who stands for the accused?" Judge Crater demanded.

"I do, your honor," Williams said.

"Who stands for the State?" Judge Crater asked, and had one
nervous second when he thought that Irad was about to stand;
but the thin man held his seat.

"I do, your honor," Sandburg declared. Crater/leLane breathed
a secret sigh of relief. If Irad had stood, he could and would have
declared him unqualified to practice law before this court and
given him a brief lecture on where and how to get his law degree
and pass the bar. But it would have raised the temper of the crowd
to have Irad so refused.

"What are the charges?" Judge Crater asked formally.

The court clerk stood, docket in hand. "The People of the Great
and Sovereign State and Independent Duchy of California versus
Mordecai Lehrer. The defendant is accused of violating the criminal statutes of this state in that he did, on the night of March

tenth, in the fourteenth year of the reign of Duke Yammoto, criminally release or cause to be released two convicted felons who were being held in the town jail prior to their execution."

LeLane stared at Mordecai while the charges were being read. Mordecai looked much older and more tired than leLane remembered, but Mordecai always looked older and tireder than he remembered.

"How do you plead?" leLane asked, beginning the litany.

Williams stood next to his client. "We plead not guilty, your honor."

"Do you wish a jury trial?"

"We agree to abide by your judgment, and we waive our right to a jury trial." So went the litany.

"Does the State agree?"

Sandburg rose in place. "The State waives its right to trial by jury."

There was a stirring in the audience, and leLane looked up. Irad had finally risen. "May I address the court?" he asked. His voice was dry, like the rattle of a snake about to strike.

"On what subject or in what capacity?" leLane asked.

"As *amicus curiae.*"

"I see. In what fashion do you propose to be a friend to this court?"

"I speak for this town," Irad said, "and the people of this town."

LeLane looked around, but none of the intent faces in the audience showed any inclination to disagree with Irad's assumption of the role of spokesman. "Go on," he said.

"The people," Irad stated, "do not waive their right to try this man, Mordecai, by a jury of his peers."

So that was it. LeLane should gave guessed. "You may speak for the people of this town," he said, leaning forward, "but I don't see how I can accept your assumption of spokesman for the Duchy of California."

"Every man is entitled to a jury trial," Irad pronounced.

"The defendant has waived his right."

"*We* are entitled to a jury trial." There was a murmur of agreement from the assemblage; the first sound they had made since the lunch break.

A riot, leLane reflected, would do none of them any good. And there was always an out, if you could find it. He turned to the court clerk. "Is there a current list of acceptable talesmen?"

"Ah," Barnaby flipped through the pages of his ledger in a panic, "let me see—give me a moment, your honor. Surely there must—"

"I have assembled such a list," Irad said.

"You have?" LeLane was not surprised.

"It is drawn from the enumeration of adults in the town ledger," Irad said. "All those known to be of good moral character were included."

"I see," leLane said. And he did.

"The list was assembled by the mayor, the sheriff, and myself."

"I see," leLane repeated, glaring at the mayor, who would not meet his eye. He was boxed. He turned to the court clerk. "Take the list and assemble the tales," he instructed.

"Sir? I mean, your honor?"

"Get all those people whose names are on the list to the court-room. How many names are there?"

"Forty-seven," Irad said.

"Take the first twenty, that should be sufficient. First call off the names out loud." LeLane turned to the audience. "If you hear your name called, stand up. Otherwise remain seated," he instructed.

Barnaby squeaked his way through the list, and the members of the audience rose one by one. When he was done, forty-four of the forty-seven people named were standing. They were all male, and none seemed younger than about forty. LeLane thought briefly of starting a women's-rights or youths'-rights movement, then decided that it would solve nothing and only cause more problems. Besides, it would take longer than ten minutes, which was about as long as he dared stall.

"The first twelve talesmen will please file into the jury box," leLane directed. "Pull that table in the corner away from the wall. I see there's twelve chairs over there already. Must be from the last time you folks needed a jury. When would that have been?"

No one even looked embarrassed, so leLane dropped that tack. But no one made a move to do anything, and Barnaby stood poised on one foot like a jogger posing for a sketch.

"What's the problem?" leLane asked.

"Judge, your honor," Barnaby said, putting his foot down, "which are the first twelve talesmen? You mean alphabetical-like?"

"I'll tell you what," leLane said, looking over the men standing, "we will be fair and impartial. Clerk, I direct you to go to the rear door and pick the twelve men standing closest to the back of the room. Gentlemen, when Barnaby here touches you, I want you to come forward and take your seats in the jury box." At least, he reflected, they're the ones who were slightly less eager to get here. Maybe that means something.

The talesmen took their seats and both attorneys agreed to waive challenges, so the twelve became a jury. The courtroom, which at no time had been noisy, became preternaturally silent again.

Now that the preliminary sparring was over, the fight itself was very short. The facts of the case were simple and easily placed in evidence by the prosecution. LeLane and his attorneys kept everything pitched at the level of a dull monotone: factual, dry, and unexciting. The defense didn't try to dispute the testimony. The audience seemed about ready to go to sleep when Irad insisted upon taking the stand. Then everyone sat up straighter and started to listen again.

"We are a God-fearing people," Irad prefaced.

"Mr.—ah—Irad," leLane said, "I'm allowing you to speak because you claim to have something to say that is relevant to the issue at trial. The fact that you may have some reason to fear the Diety is beyond the scope of this court, and whom you profess to speak for beyond yourself is a bit vague to the court. Is that the regal 'we,' the editorial 'we,' or do you have a tapeworm?"

Irad turned to stare full-face at Judge Crater. The wrath of the righteous burned on his lips, and he was about to spit fire at he who had lit the match. He opened his mouth. . . .

"Contempt of court," Sandburg sidled over to him to whisper, "is punishable by a fine of up to five thousand Washington dollars and a sentence of up to five years in the state penitentiary on Alcatraz Island."

Irad continued to glare, but he glared silently. For a long minute he held this pose, then he turned back to the audience.

"Four score years ago," he announced, "the sons of Adam numbered a multitude on the face of the Earth. . . ."

"Sir," leLane said.

"Now the purposes of the Lord are not for Man to know, and yet his message is clear to those who would read the Book. Idolatry and sin must be wiped out."

"That is beyond the jurisdiction of this court," leLane said, interrupting firmly. "I'm sorry, Mr. Irad, but you are going to have to be pertinent to the cause at hand. I cannot allow you to use this courtroom as a stage for your religious sentiments; they are better stated elsewhere."

"I shall pertain," Irad said. "If you'll be good enough to let me continue for a moment.

"Our babies are dying again. The plague that was visited upon us over seven decades ago, the Death, is threatening to return. Why? What is the Good Lord trying to tell us?"

"Enough of that!" leLane said. "You seem unable to confine your remarks to the case being tried, so I am going to have to ask you to step down. Thank you very much for trying to help."

"I have more to say!" Irad insisted.

"I have ordered you to step down," leLane told him. "Do you wish to stand in contempt of this court?"

Irad shook his head and stared at the jury. "No, your honor. I will step down. But these people here, they know what I'm trying to say."

And Irad was right. The jury deliberated for ten minutes. Mordecai was guilty.

"The defendant will please rise," leLane said.

Mordecai pulled himself to his feet.

"You have been judged guilty of diverse crimes against the state of California by a jury of your peers. Have you anything to say before I pronounce sentence?"

"Nothing, your honor."

"Mordecai Lehrer, I hereby sentence you to be taken from here to the state penitentiary at Alcatraz Island, where you are to be incarcerated for a term to be established at the People's pleasure, but not to be less than ten years."

Mordecai buried his head in his hands and his shoulders began to shake silently.

The audience nodded and whispered quietly among themselves. This was justice. This was Law. Only Irad looked displeased.

Judge Crater and his entourage rode slowly out of town that evening. Two days later a state-police car, in perfect condition except for the wooden wheels on the hundred-year-old axles, was pulled into town by two large grays. Two men in blue accepted custody of Mordecai and hustled him off to his fate.

6.

~~~~~~~~~~

"I'll go," Mordecai insisted. "I can't stay around here anyway."

"It's not that simple," leLane told him. "What are you going to do; jump on your mule and ride off into the night?"

"I've got this wagon—"

"Not big enough. Besides, by now every town for miles around has heard of your trial. You want to get arrested for breaking jail?"

Mordecai smiled. "Not again," he said. "But still I volunteer to go. I belong in motion. I feel better with wheels under me, ah, feet."

They were sitting in the common room of the Palisades Enclave, at a table in one corner. Not exactly celebrating, just relaxing in each other's company.

"Decent men," leLane said, scowling at Mordecai's empty glass, "who respect the effort and time that an old friend has taken to save his—their—lives; these men have the courtesy to drink their host's wine. Particularly when said host is identical to said life-saving old friend."

"I dare you to repeat that," Mordecai said, refilling his glass from the decanter of red. "Tell me more about this expedition."

"The exclave has agreed—"

"One step back, old friend. What is an exclave?"

"Ah. The various New York City enclaves—Columbia and NYU and those—have formed one large group to insure domestic tranquility, provide for the common defense, promote the general welfare, and gather the largest Golden Age artifact collection in the world. It is to be the depository of all the world's knowledge, to be held for such a time as we are able to make use of it again. Sort of high-class packrats."

"I should think," Mordecai said, "that the best safeguard for the Wisdom of the Ancients would be wide dispersal."

"And so should I," leLane agreed. "But it makes sense to have one central place where all the duplicates are stored for ready reference."

"Then they just want a, so to speak, duplicate collection?"

"No. They want whatever we'll send them. What we're sending is a microfiche collection of the school's library: five hundred thousand volumes in two large trunks."

"So. It sounds like a worthwhile job. Let me make the trip."

"You don't really know what you're asking," leLane said. "We're making a special wagon to haul the stuff. And getting a large wagon across the continent is a major undertaking."

"And too tough for an old man; is that what's on your mind?"

"Mordecai, I have no idea how old you are, and I'm not going to ask. But, truthfully, I can't think of anything that I consider you too old for. Anything. Give us a couple of days to decide what we're going to do about this wagon and how we're going to do it."

Mordecai considered this as he slowly sipped his wine. When the glass was empty he stood up, pulled a comb from his pocket and ran it through his hair and beard, nodded to leLane, and then walked very carefully to his room.

The next day Peter and Ruth came to sit with Mordecai in the dining hall as he was contemplating his lunch. "We want to find some way to thank you," Peter said.

Mordecai looked at the two of them for a moment and smiled. "English," he said, "is the best way."

"But—" Peter said.

Ruth laid her hand on his arm to silence him. "Thank you," she said quietly to Mordecai.

After lunch Peter and Ruth took Mordecai on a tour of the enclave campus and told him about life amid the remains of an antique university. Mordecai, in turn, told them stories about the life of a peddler and about the different towns and enclaves that he visited on his circuit. To the towns he was a peddler, to the enclaves he was a part of their special courier service.

"It must be an exciting life," Peter commented.

Mordecai thought back on what he had said, trying to figure out what they found exciting. "I've never thought of it in those terms," he said. "There is a certain sameness to it after twenty years. I'm a messenger, a peddler, a dealer in pins and needles, pots and pans, yardgoods and ready made. My mercantile life is interesting at times, frightening at times, and at times as monotonous as the gait of my mule; but I wouldn't have called it exciting. The work I do for the enclaves is important, but I wouldn't call it exciting. If the townspeople had ever suspected, that would be a different matter; but they never did."

A whistle sounded from somewhere around them: three short blasts repeated three times.

"Come on!" Peter said, taking Mordecai's arm and urging him toward a large white building. "That's the general call."

"The what?" Mordecai asked, allowing himself to be urged. "Should I be alarmed?"

"No, no," Ruth said. "That's the signal for everyone to gather in the auditorium. The danger signal, the one we call 'battle stations,' is a continuous series of bleeps that goes on for three minutes or until the whistle runs out of steam; whichever happens first."

"Fine," Mordecai said. "Now I understand: we proceed, but we are not alarmed."

The auditorium still had a deserted look when they walked in. But then, the presence of all four hundred residents of the Palisades Enclave would have left the room slightly less than one-fifth full. A group of about ten people were sitting behind a long table on the stage.

"Look," Peter said, nodding his chin at the stage, "they're all there."

"All of them?" Mordecai asked, looking with interest at the group as they found seats.

"All the brass," Peter explained. "Say, where'd that expression come from? Why 'brass'? Why not gold or silver, or even iron?"

"It dates back to the Etruscan Army, where only the officers had brass shields," explained Mordecai, who had a fondness for instant history.

"What sort of shields did the soldiers carry?" Ruth asked.

"Leather," Mordecai said firmly.

Joseph leLane, acting head of the Table of Deans, rapped a soup spoon against the table for silence. "We seem to be here, mostly," he said. "Please move forward and take seats in the front of the room. None of us feel like yelling."

The gathering grouped closer around the stage. Everyone, both on the platform and off, looked very somber. "Say," Mordecai whispered to Peter, "just how serious is one of these meetings?"

"I don't know," Peter said. "We've never had one before, that I can remember."

"Ah!" Mordecai said. He settled back in his chair and prepared himself for the unknown.

LeLane came forward to the foot of the stage and stared into the auditorium with an unfocused gaze. "I'll make it brief," he said. "We felt you should know as soon as possible. I don't know why, actually, as there's nothing any of us can do—" he paused, groping for words, and finally finished, "but we thought you should know."

The audience collectively seemed to hold its breath, waiting, Mordecai thought, for the other shoe to fall.

"We have received," leLane said, leaning back against the table, "a long bulletin from Radio Chicago. It's a report on their latest communication with Ley Base on Mars. It contains a copy of the actual message from Mars and a fair amount of commentary. The message, however, is self-explanatory."

Everyone in the audience turned to stare at his neighbor, to see if anyone else had a notion of why any happening at Ley Base, on the planet Mars, would be of such immediate concern to them. Nobody did. They turned back to leLane.

"Ley Base has been continuing research on the ECHO virus mutation that caused the pandemic—the Death—seventy years ago. They have maintained the high technological base that Earth had then. They've had to on Mars; without it they'd perish. It's the Death itself that has isolated them. Even before we on Earth lost the capability, we had to stop sending manned flights to Mars. The presence of one Earthman on Mars would sentence the colony to the Death: to lose over ninety per cent of its population to the virus, and then the rest because they'd be unable to keep the life-support systems going.

"A couple of drone flights—carefully sterilized—had cultures of the virus as a part of their cargo. This was to give them a chance to develop a defense against it; something no laboratory on Earth had been able to do. Also to try to determine if the mutation was indeed man-made, as was rumored at the time. This has never been either proved or disproved."

LeLane paused and looked around. His audience was politely interested and vaguely puzzled. "They've been working on the disease these past years. As far as we know, no group on Earth is conducting such research now. For one thing, the biological technology ain't around no more. For another, there's no point: if you're alive, you're immune.

"Now for the message." LeLane held a yellow piece of paper in front of him and read from it evenly: "'Our continuing research into the mutated ECHO virus that is responsible for the disease known as the Death shows the existence of a secondary mutation, which has a fifty per cent chance of occurring spontaneously within a hundred thousand generations. This new form of the virus is invariably fatal to all tested rodents and primates, even those immune to the primary form. It does not affect dogs, cats, or cattle. It has not been tested on humans. Statistical analysis indicates that if, as is probable, it is also fatal to humans, the population base on Earth is still large enough to support a pandemic. This would, effectively, destroy what remains of civilization and ninety to ninety-five per cent of humanity.

"'According to our best available models, the pandemic will occur at an originating site in North America or Europe in not less than twenty or more than thirty years. We have insufficient data on population density or distribution over the rest of Earth.'"

LeLane paused and looked out at his silent audience. "That's the bad news; now for the good. . . ."

That did it. The assemblage broke out into a babble. No one screamed, no one fainted, no one even audibly cursed, but suddenly everyone wanted to speak at once. If mankind is going to die, it's going to go down talking.

LeLane had to rap his spoon on the table for silence. "I'm not finished yet," he told them. "There *is* good news, of a sort. It presents a few interesting problems, but it rates as good news.

"There's a vaccine against this new virus. It is over eighty per cent effective in populations of animals that have survived the first version of the Death. Unfortunately for Ley Base, the vaccine itself would be fatal to anyone who has not contracted the Death and survived; so it's not the answer they're looking for. But if they can get a sample to Earth, it could save the human race.

"And so a ship will be on its way within a month. If it makes it to the space station, and if the shuttle out there is still operable, we'll have a sample of the vaccine within five months. Chicago is going to handle the recovery of the shuttle by reactivating, as best they can, Lincoln Spaceport. All enclaves are asked to set up facilities to produce this vaccine. Since we still have the rudiments of a biology department here, we're to produce a handbook to teach the others what to do and distribute it as widely as possible. Now you can talk."

〜〜〜〜〜〜〜

7

It was a cold, damp night. The steady rain above translated, down on the subway platform, into a chorus of drips that echoed and re-echoed down the black tunnel that pierced the station end to end. Cadet-Sergeant-Designate Wail, a tall, thin, melancholy youth, walked his assigned post along the platform as silently as possible, listening, shivering, and cursing the fate—and the lieutenant—who had put his name at that exact spot in the guard roster.

Wail kept his mind busy by examining the stupidity of his superiors for assuming that a group of vandals would ever think of attacking the exclave down the ancient subway tunnel. Periodically he froze and listened to the faint sounds that his active mind interpreted as that vandal horde attacking. So far the noises had turned out to be no more than rats, mice, or imagination; but this was reassuring only between sounds.

As Wail walked he made up a short poem about his lieutenant; a verse he would never dare write down. Then he heard another noise. He froze. Then he realized that this time it was the steady tramp of the corporal of the guard approaching with his relief. He hurried over to the wide gate that was his exit to the upstairs world and stood waiting as they approached. "Halt!" he called. "Who goes there?"

They halted. "Corporal of the guard, with the relief," the corporal called back, opening the shutter on his bull's-eye lantern enough to reveal himself and his companion.

"Advance!"

The corporal advanced and halted again, completing the next position in this age-old military minuet.

Wail brought his carbine to a snappy position of present arms, and the corporal returned the salute. "You are relieved," the corporal said. He then did a formal about-face and barked, "Post!" to the relief. The three of them then finished the dance, and Wail marched off behind the corporal.

When they reached street level the corporal abruptly stopped, causing Wail to do a clumsy two-step to avoid running into him. "Relax, Wail," the corporal said. "Your two hours is up. You're off duty."

"It's amazing how time flies when you're having fun," Wail said, slinging the carbine over his shoulder, muzzle down.

"Let's just saunter back to the guardhouse slowly, you and I," the corporal said, "and have a little talk."

"Fine," Wail said, feeling the fine drizzle against his face. But officer candidates were supposed to ignore rain, and so he let the drops form and run down his chin. Corporal Hesperson was not a particular friend of his, but for that matter he had no particular friends. "What are we going to talk about?"

Corporal Hesperson gave a vague shrug and looked uncomfortable. "I've been asked to talk to you, you know. It's your attitude. Not that I give a damn, you understand. Like I said, I've been asked. . . ."

They slowly walked down the street, and Corporal Hesperson searched for words. Wail looked up at the ancient buildings towering over them, great dead monuments to the dead past, and felt that he didn't care what Hesperson had to say.

"You ask too many questions," Hesperson explained finally.

"Is that bad, asking questions?" Wail asked.

Hesperson smiled. "Is that a question?" Wail didn't smile back and didn't answer, and Hesperson erased his smile. "Not information questions," he said. "Meddlesome questions." He shook his head. "Wail, you're developing the reputation of being a troublemaker. And I don't mean just in the ROTC. I'm sure you don't intend to make a career of this chickenshit; just get your commission when you graduate, serve your five years, and get out; like me."

Hesperson waited for some sort of comment, but Wail merely stared straight ahead silently. "This wasn't my idea, you know," Hesperson said. "I mean, we're not close friends or anything. But they decided that someone had to talk to you, and I am your superior officer—in the cadet corps, at least."

Wail looked down at him. "They?"

"I mean, we're both sergeants-designate, but I'm an acting corporal. And besides, you're only designate because of your test scores, and if you keep up like this you'll get passed over again."

"Everyone gets passed over his first time on the list," Wail said. "And you keep getting passed over until they need a sergeant."

"Sure," Hesperson said. "Only some people don't ever make it. And then they graduate and spend five years as second lieutenants because nobody needs first lieutenants, except other people make captain."

"Who's the 'they'?"

"And then when you get out, you spend another five years as a research assistant before you make assistant professor, and you never quite get your Ph.D. or are allowed to do original research, because, after all, someone has to teach class—and you're so good at it."

"Who told you to talk to me?"

"You want to get somewhere in the exclave, you got to have friends—friends with rank. My father retired just two years ago. You know what he retired as?"

Wail shook his head. "No."

"He was an assistant professor. In charge of cataloging portable radios. After thirty years. Portable radios, by God! As though there were anything to listen to."

They were in front of the main entrance now. Here some of the precious electrical power from the generator in the second basement was squandered, and two dim bulbs lit up the large, arched doorway. A massive shaft of white oak stood beneath the center of the arch, bearing, carved into its face, the new identity of the building.

EXCLAVE
formerly:
Barnard College
City University of New York
Columbia University
Cooper Union

Fordham University
Hunter College
Manhattan College
New York University
Pratt Institute
Rockefeller University
THE PAST IS PRESERVED

And above, carved into the stone of the arch, its past:

350 *Fifth Avenue* = = THE EMPIRE STATE BUILDING.

"Come on," Corporal Hesperson said. "Let's get out of this rain."

"Who told you to talk to me?" Wail asked again, as they pushed through the doors. "Why didn't they talk to my faculty advisor?" The door guard nodded recognition to them as they passed her. They nodded back.

"As a matter of fact," Hesperson said, "it was your faculty advisor asked me to talk to you. Said he keeps getting these reports about you. Kind of low-key griping, you know? Like you're more interested in writing poetry than collecting or cataloging. Is that right? You write poetry?"

"Anything wrong with that?" Wail asked aggressively.

Hesperson shrugged. "I don't care, but your advisor is sure unhappy about it. You know the bit: 'The business of the exclave is saving the past for the future.' Like the monasteries during the Dark Ages. Remember, those monks were supposed to copy poetry, not write it."

They walked upstairs to the third floor, across the hall of washing machines and driers, to the off-duty guard's room, and Hesperson flopped on a cot. "Think on what I've been saying."

Wail sat down on a hardback chair and stared off into space. "You ever wonder what it was like?" he asked.

"What?"

"The Golden Age. Before the Death."

"Across the river," Hesperson volunteered, "they call it the Evil Time, or the Time of Sodom."

"You'd have your own little house," Wail mused, "with your wife and family. You'd go to a job every morning and spend the day making washing machines or refrigerators or portable radios or automobiles—they sure as hell made a lot of automobiles—and then come home at night. You'd reach into your own refrigerator for a soft drink—"

"What's that?"

"The stuff that was in all those bottles up on the nineteenth. Or a beer—"

"I know what that is. Want to go down and get a bucket? I'll go half."

"On duty?"

"Yeah—that's right. Forget it."

Wail lay down on a cot next to Hesperson and they both stared at the ceiling. Hesperson's gaze shifted to the near wall, where an ancient centerfold from a long-defunct magazine was pasted and shellacked. Wail fell asleep.

8.

〜〜〜〜〜〜〜

It looked like an unhappy cross between a covered wagon and a circus van: large cross-springs pushing it high off the axles, high board sides with no slope, flat bowed arches spaced close together supporting the heavy canvas top. The axles were steel and seemed too small for the vehicle. They terminated in metal wheels with rubber tires. From whiffletree to centerboard it seemed to cant slightly to the left; from centerboard to tailgate the cant somehow shifted to the right. It was inelegant. It was awkward-looking. But it was the best effort of the wainwrights of Palisades Enclave.

Mordecai looked it over critically. "You're not going to send the kid up in a crate like that?" he asked leLane.

"What are you talking about?" leLane demanded.

"Never mind," Mordecai said. "Just put it down to an obscure fondness for antique remarks. So this is the vehicle in which you expect me to cross the country?"

LeLane nodded. "Wainwrightery—is that a word?—anyway, wainwrightery is pretty much of a forgotten art, like designing pinball machines or playing the electronic raisin."

Mordecai stared at leLane, then shook his head. "I won't ask."

"It's some sort of musical instrument. It takes up a whole floor of the music building, with a room the size of a small theater for the controls. We have a whole library of records made on it, and some of them are quite intriguing. But no living man has any idea of how to make the thing work. We diverted the power from the physics building one evening and turned it on. It hummed a lot, and then it screeched, and then it howled, and then it died."

"I'm glad I asked," Mordecai said. "Put your wainwrights on it; maybe all it needs are wheels and a canvas top." He walked slowly around the ungainly vehicle, methodically kicking each tire as he came to it. "They're too small," he said. "It's not traditional. The wheels are supposed to stick out on the sides of the wagon. Great wooden wheels with dozens of spokes."

"Rubber tires are in right now," leLane said. "Take my word for it."

"Suppose I have a flat?"

"You'll have a spare tire, a patch kit, and a hand pump."

"Splendid. Hundred-year-old tires, a patch kit, and a hand pump."

"These are among the last usable rubber tires in the world," leLane said, kneeling down and running his hand around the visible tread of the left front tire. "They were packed to be sent up to the Arctic and stored for future use, but they were never sent. I don't think anyone could have anticipated their use quite this far in the future. Be careful when you get to the exclave, or the dons will rip them right off the wagon for display."

"I would think there would be a lot of unused tires," Mordecai commented. "The Death hit so fast they didn't have time to use up anything."

"Rubber rots in air, even the artificial rubber used in these tires. Even without air it rots; it rots more slowly, but it rots. Twenty or thirty years is the outside shelf life of a tire. Even with these, if you were going any faster than a horse, I wouldn't trust them."

"Well, let's hope I don't have a blowout. I may be the last man on Earth to change a tire."

"That's a strange notion."

"Yes. You know, they used to make up books of 'firsts'; perhaps the time has come for us to assemble a book of 'lasts': last changed tire, last flown airplane—I wonder when that was—last electric light, last appendix operation, last election, last literate man. All coming up, I'm afraid."

"If we live that long," leLane said cheerfully.

"Ah, yes," Mordecai said. "And what are we doing about our impending doom?"

"The booklet is written, and being printed even now. It gives complete instructions for setting up a lab to grow the vaccine, when and if we get it. There are also kits being made up with samples of the hardware needed."

"Great," Mordecai said. "When do I go?"

"As soon as possible. We figure you should have a crew of two to aid you. You're the captain, of course; you have more experience at this sort of thing than the rest of us."

"Of course," Mordecai nodded. "That's what we old men have: experience."

"We'll ask for volunteers to accompany you tomorrow; warning them about the hardships involved and your sense of humor. You can weed from those who apply, if any."

"I've weeded already. Peter Thrumager and Ruth McEwan."

The expression on leLane's face very carefully didn't change. "Peter and Ruth?"

Mordecai grinned. "I think I've surprised you. Yes: they asked me yesterday, and I told them I'd think about it. I did."

"You're joking. I mean, it's your choice, of course, if they did volunteer." LeLane busied himself checking the tiedowns for the canvas. He went down to the front, around the far side of the wagon, across the back, and returned to where Mordecai was standing. "They're children. I thought you wanted adults."

"They're adults by the standards of this community," Mordecai said very seriously. "I've thought it out. You want to maximize the chances of getting this wagon across country?"

"I haven't told you this," leLane said, "I didn't think I had to: I estimate your odds of making it all the way across at something around twenty per cent."

"You're in the odds business," Mordecai said. "I'm in the wagon-driving business."

"So?"

"You're right. You're probably overgenerous. In these fragmented times the chances for survival outside of your group— whatever group that is—are slim. And six months on the road is pushing the odds. But if this is worth doing at all, it's worth doing well. That's my original thought for the day."

"How does taking Peter and Ruth in lieu of two more adult members of the enclave community constitute doing anything well? I ask in sincere curiosity, secure in the knowledge that you'll have a brilliant answer."

Mordecai climbed up into the driver's seat of the wagon and

sat. "A bit hard for three thousand miles," he said. "What about a cushion? At any rate, as for the choice of Peter and Ruth; I have devised a persona, a disguise, in which we are to travel. Peter and Ruth would be excellent as my assistants. At this particular juncture in the affairs of man, those of us who are given something useful to do—or something we can feel is useful—no matter how dangerous—no matter what our age—are the lucky ones."

"Let's hear the scheme," leLane said, sitting resignedly on a convenient cask.

Mordecai looked down at him. "It will demand a bit of preparation, a little painting and carpentry on the wagon, a little rehearsing, a few props—"

"You're not going as a theater troupe?"

"Close, but no cigar, as they used to say at carnivals."

"What then?"

"Snake oil."

LeLane thought about that for a minute. "You've conveyed no useful information," he decided. "It sounds like an obscure ethnic expletive."

"We're going to sell snake oil. We're going to be a traveling medicine show, the like of which this country hasn't seen in the past couple of hundred years."

"Snake oil?"

"As I understand it, that's a sort of generic description for the medicine-man's elixir. Guaranteed, as the man says, to cure everything from lumbago to warts. Good for what ails you. The more you drink, the better you get. Great stuff, whatever it is."

They discussed it for the next three days, during which time Mordecai did not win leLane over, but leLane did not come up with anything better.

"We'll have to use up precious room in the wagon for your store of bottles or boxes or whatever you sell," leLane pointed out.

"It'll minimize the chance of getting hijacked," Mordecai said. "Everyone will know we carry nothing of value and little of interest."

"You'll have to stop every three miles to pitch your product—it will slow you down."

"We'll be accepted wherever we stop," Mordecai replied. "They'll look down at us as traveling showmen—one step worse than peddlers and one step better than beggars—but they won't be afraid of us, and probably will leave us alone. And we don't have to stop if we don't want to—nobody will notice if we don't."

"Wouldn't you rather have two adult helpers?"

"They're both of age. Innocence is a virtue in the snake-oil trade. Besides, I need a beautiful young lady for the act."

"What sort of act?" leLane asked suspiciously.

"Don't worry, it's all proper and moral and decent. Perhaps a bit suggestive, but in such a way that the dirty old men will be sure that the thoughts originated in their minds without any help from us."

"You think those kids will be good at that?"

Mordecai looked disappointed. "Joe," he said, "they don't have to be very good, just reasonably convincing. We're not really trying to sell the stuff, remember?"

LeLane finally capitulated. "It's your wagon, or will be when it leaves here. Whatever you think best, is best."

"What about Peter and Ruth?"

"I'm not happy about their going," leLane said. "But I can't stop them, and I certainly won't try. What color do you want the wagon painted?"

"I want the canvas two-sided," Mordecai said. "Dull on one side and bright on the other. So when we travel, we don't stand out; and when we stop, we do. Big blocks of primary color for the bright side, I think. I was thinking of something like a scene of Lazarus being raised from the dead; kind of a giant mural running along the canvas front to back, but I decided against it."

"Lucky thing. Our mural painter won't be available for other commissions until he finishes the ceiling of our chapel. You'll have to settle for bright blotches by our amateurs."

One side of the wagon was converted into a sliding platform that could be pulled out to form a stage and hitched back to the wagon's side in five minutes. Then the wagon was painted and the microfiche records and various artifacts to be transported were brought aboard and stowed.

"Say," leLane said one morning after breakfast, "just what sort of snake oil are you going to peddle?"

"I have given it considerable thought," Mordecai informed him. "My first idea was to merely pick something entirely innocuous, like ninety-proof alcohol flavored with cloves. Then I found a couple of giant stored tins of aspirin in your medical supply."

"Our ancestors must have lived on it," leLane said. "We must have a couple of hundred pounds of pills in the warehouse."

"We'll take one of those giant cans, dissolve the pills in liquid. Make it up in strength about a quarter gram per teaspoonful, and we've got a useful, comparatively safe medication. At that strength, downing a whole bottle shouldn't do much damage."

A large supply of four-fluid-ounce brown glass bottles was discovered in the basement of the chemistry building and donated to the cause, but the stoppers proved to be a problem.

"Why can't you just give out pills?" leLane asked as he disgustedly rubbed an ancient hard-rubber stopper back and forth in his hand and watched it crumble.

"You're the psychologist," Mordecai said. "You should be the one who tells me that pills are a symbol of the hated and feared Golden Age, and would be mistrusted to the point of danger to the distributor. I'm sure you would use more psychological terms to tell me this, but—"

"I don't think I'm sorry I asked," leLane said, "but I know I'm damn sure I'm sorry you answered. My training as a psychologist is what enables me to know my own mind well enough to tell you this. Remember, I haven't been out peddling around the countryside for the past forty years. I've been stuck here in this ivory tower with the rotten plumbing."

Carved wooden stoppers dipped in melted wax to make them airtight when tapped into the bottles proved to be the most sensible answer to the corkage problem. But there were other problems.

"What sort of show?" Peter asked Mordecai.

"What's that?" Mordecai responded, looking up from the list he was compiling.

"What sort of show? What are you doing?"

"Making a list."

"Of what?"

"What we need to take."

"Oh. What do we need to take?"

"Well . . ." Mordecai waved the list. "Here's four feet of what we need, and I'm not done yet. It's the little things. . . . Now what was that?"

"What I asked you was: What sort of show? What are we going to be doing?" Peter looked very serious. "Ruth and I want to rehearse."

"Ah, yes!" Mordecai considered, his right hand tugging at his beard. "The show. The show! Now, what sort of show? What do we want it to accomplish? It must entertain without offending, encourage emotion without allowing thought; create, in short, a willing suspension of disbelief. I do not think the classical dramatists have anything for us. We should not toy with morality plays. Besides, we'll be passing through areas where we have no idea of what the prevailing morality is. No; all in all I think we must go back to basics. Peter, my lad, how would you like to be the dog-faced boy?"

"The what?"

"Ruth might make a good ape-lady. I shall think on it. Perhaps we'd better leave the two-headed baby out."

"Far out," Peter agreed. "I know I'm only a private in this army, and it isn't my place to ask questions, but what are you talking about? What's this about dogs and gorillas and two-headed children?"

"It's what we're going to do, Peter. We haven't the experience or the time to put on a show, in the regular sense of the word; so we're going to give an exhibition."

"Can't we manage something better than a phony freak show?" Ruth asked.

"Well," Mordecai considered, "there's magic; that always goes over big. But it's easier to manufacture a dog head than a set of magical apparatus."

"I think I can help you there," Ruth said. "Come with me." She led them down into a basement of the humanities building and into a storeroom. It was filled from floor to ceiling with trunks, except for a corridor barely wide enough to squeeze into sideways.

Mordecai lighted a kerosene lantern in the hall and brought it into the storeroom. "What's all this?" he asked, holding the lantern before him and peering at the dust-covered trunks. Everything was covered with at least an inch of dust, except for one corner that looked comparatively clean. Peter tried blowing the dust off the surface of one trunk and almost choked on the cloud he raised.

"Careful!" Mordecai said, looking up from the small box he was gingerly examining. "You must be more respectful of dust. Take it up with a damp something-or-other, or see if you can borrow the vacuum cleaner from the workshop—and a long enough extension cord to work it here, since there's no current in this wing."

"It's my discovery," Ruth said. "I used to play down here." She blew the dust off one of the almost-clean boxes and pointed to the lid. Mordecai peered down at it.

"McGinty, Haemlin & Dammeschif," he read from a large label that appeared under the dust. "The great M.H. & D. Traveling Circus & International Menagerie. Trunk 23—costumes."

"I'm fascinated," Mordecai said. "What's in them?"

"I've only opened a couple," Ruth told him. "There are all sorts of costumes, tons of strange apparatus, and giant posters. I tried getting more of them opened, but they were rusted shut and I was afraid to damage them. I kept hoping I'd find an elephant in one. I was very small."

"It sounds like a worthwhile hope," Mordecai told her, "regardless of your age.

"Okay, you two, get a bucket of water, a bunch of rags, and a can of oil. We're going to go through these trunks and bring McGinty, Haemlin, and Dammeschif back to life again. You found magical apparatus?" he asked Ruth.

"I wouldn't know magical apparatus if it bit me," Ruth said. "But I found a clipping book that described them as a traveling magical show of the quality of Houdini or Carter. I left it on a shelf—here." She pulled a thick, wide book off a shelf and handed it to Mordecai.

Mordecai gently laid it on the ground and opened it, under the eye of the kerosene lantern. In a faded elegant hand on the inside of the front cover was written: *Waggoner & Johnson— write-ups—fifth book—July 1920—October 1922.*

"Over a hundred and sixty years ago," Peter said with a mild note of awe in his voice. They turned the pages and saw photographs of two well-dressed men sawing a woman in half, floating a woman in mid-air, and performing other acts of mayhem upon their female assistants.

"Marvelous," Mordecai said. "Let's get these trunks cleaned off and opened up."

After enough of a mopping up to keep the dust from flying every time someone breathed, Peter went around and oiled the hinges on the more accessible trunks. Then they sat back to allow the oil time to penetrate the hundred years of rust. "How do you figure these things got here?" Peter asked.

"Universities collect strange things," Mordecai said. "Something about taxes. It was before my time."

When he couldn't wait any longer, Peter took a screwdriver and went to work on the lid of the nearest trunk. With a little effort he was able to crack the lid and swing it open. A strong, musty smell immediately invaded the room, but by some miracle the costumes which filled the trunk seemed to be in fairly good condition. They were of heavy fabrics, brightly colored, and stiff with age. Some of them seemed permanently folded, flattened, creased, and wrinkled to the point where they could not be separated front from back without fear of tearing the material. But others looked as though they could be shaken out and hung up today, then put on tomorrow.

Peter pushed his arms into the sleeves of a bright red cossack's jacket with large gold buttons and fastened it around him. "How do I look?" he demanded. "I think it's a bit large."

"The world hasn't seen your like," Mordecai told him, "in a hundred years." He looked around the room once more and sniffed. "I can see," he told the world at large, "that it's time for me to practice my juggling once again."

~~~~~~~~~~~~~~~~~

9

It was two more weeks before they were ready to leave. The project, which had been of only peripheral interest to the rest of the enclave community, seemed to take on more and more importance as they prepared to go. Every day someone would approach one of the three travelers with some carefully contrived item or carefully thought out suggestion that might be of use on the trip.

"You've become a symbol," leLane told Mordecai when they both noted what was happening. "This trip is Palisades Enclave's contribution toward the future of the human race."

"Or toward construction of its mausoleum," Mordecai said sourly. "So some race of giant grasshoppers can land here in a couple of thousand years and see what us apes were like."

The biology booklets and kits were packed into the wall of the wagon, along the bottom. A surplus of two thousand booklets were packed at the bottom of a trunk for general distribution, as Mordecai saw fit. "This will probably be the best-distributed book in the past fifty years," leLane said.

"Great," Mordecai said, lashing the trunk into place. "Just call me Johnny pamphlet-seed. How is that Martian planning to get down here to Earth anyhow? If I remember what I learned in my youth, those Mars ships were not made for atmosphere landings."

"You weren't listening," leLane said. "There's a shuttle in orbit. Been there since the last flight."

"That was over seventy years ago," Mordecai said.

"The only thing that could decay is the orbit itself," leLane told him. "But if the ship is still up there, it's probably still good. Everything would be sitting there at close to absolute zero, waiting for someone to come along and turn the heater back on."

"Then you think his chances are good?"

"No. There's too much that can go wrong. I think his chances are lousy. Whoever our Martian friend is, I think he's a very brave man. Six months' isolation in space, then a quick drop in an antique ship, for the privilege of landing on Earth and risking a ninety per cent chance of being dead in three weeks."

"I thought Chicago was going to try to get him back to orbit again."

LeLane shrugged. "They're going to try."

"They probably had to draw straws on Mars to pick among the volunteers," Mordecai said. "People are like that. Unfortunately, people are also like a good many other things when it suits them." He kicked at the trunk and at a barrel lashed next to it. "That's it," he said. "Unless you come up with some other bright notion, we're packed and ready to go."

Mordecai climbed down and stood next to leLane for a minute, staring at the wagon speculatively. Then he went into the dining room and gathered together eight men who were lingering over their meal. He placed four on each side of the wagon and had them rock it from side to side to the point of tipping for about ten minutes. "Thank you, gentlemen," he said when he stopped them. "I don't want to test to destruction; that's quite good enough. The wagon didn't collapse and the load didn't shift, and I'll settle for that."

"What more could you want?" asked leLane, who had aided in the jouncing.

"Well," Mordecai considered, "better stability, for one thing: the center of gravity is entirely too high for safety. Tighter springs, for another: when that wagon goes over rough ground it's going to set up a lamentable bouncing and joggling. I hear that's bad for the kidneys; and a man my age is lucky to have any kidneys left at all. Better cured wood is a third; or perhaps what I want is harder wood, or softer wood—at any rate more supple wood that doesn't creak so much when it takes a load. That creaking sound will drive me either deaf or crazy before we reach Great Salt Lake."

"We'll take your suggestions into account when we design next year's model," leLane said.

The next morning two of the enclave's strongest, most dependable horses were hitched in the traces and a third was tied on a follow-halter to the rear. The trek to the skeleton of what had been New York City, and to the exclave nestled among the bones, was about to begin. Mordecai threw the suitcase containing all the personal belongings he wanted to take with him into the back of the wagon and then went wandering off on a sudden impulse to say good-bye to his mule. Peter and Ruth were saying their private good-byes. The unspoken importance that the journey had assumed was shown in a backward way by the fact that no one came out to wave them on their way when they had actually boarded the wagon, but almost everyone in the enclave was watching from a distance at different points on the road. Only leLane was there to solemnly shake hands with each of them and silently turn around and walk off before the wagon started moving.

"What's that?" Ruth asked, indicating the canvas-wrapped bundle Mordecai had brought out with him.

"Shotgun," Mordecai said.

"Think we'll need it?" she asked.

"Yes," Mordecai said. He flicked out the two pair of reins and released the brake. The horses pulled, the wagon creaked, the wheels started to turn, and the road began passing under the show.

~~~~~~~~~~~~~~~~~~

The first two hundred miles was the easiest. The Central Valley was like an oven during the day, but it was flat, the road was smooth, and the nights were cool. They fell quickly into a routine: rising at dawn and getting underway, stopping before noon for a couple of hours to let the animals rest in whatever shade was around, and then traveling until dusk. At night they tethered the horses and went to sleep in light sleeping bags by the side of the wagon. The first night they had hobbled the horses and set them loose in a field, but the distant howling of coyotes had spooked the animals and they had had to spend half the next day rounding them up, despite the hobbles. For some reason buried deep in the equine psychology, being tethered gave the horses a sense of security and kept them quiet.

The road they were following, the road they intended to travel for three thousand miles, was the northern route of the old interstate highway system; at one time a four-lane, controlled-access superhighway, it was now an eighty-foot-wide ribbon of cracked and buckled concrete that bifurcated the continent.

They followed Route 680 up the east coast of San Francisco Bay to the Carquinez Strait at Martinez. There the road ended abruptly at the ruins of the Martinez-Benicia Bridge. To the west of the ruined bridge, close enough to be in its morning shadow, a wooden dock had been constructed. A hard-packed dirt road led from the ancient highway to the dock. On the dock, beneath a crudely lettered sign that read MARTINEZ CABLE FERRY—A. PONTINEREZ PROP., a four-horse freight wagon squatted patiently, awaiting the ferry.

Mordecai turned his team onto the dirt road and guided the wagon down to the ferry landing. When he had pulled up behind the freight wagon, Peter and Ruth climbed down to inspect the workings of the Pontinerez Proprietary Ferry. To their left, as they faced the water, a pair of mules plodded around in a tight circle on a wooden platform, hitched to the crossbars of a standing winch. A chain drive below the platform attached the winch to a large drum, which was slowly winding in a four-inch hemp rope.

At the other end of the rope, now about halfway across the half-mile strait and getting oh-so-slowly closer, was the large, flat, square platform that was the Martinez Ferry Barge. From a pair of platforms, one on each side, the two cables ran; the one on the far side being let out slowly as the near one was pulled in. This kept the unwieldy craft more or less in line, allowing for the effects of current or tide. A third, "safety," cable stretched from the center pier of the ruined bridge, split into a Y, and fastened to each end of the platform.

Peter listened to the rope creak as it went around the pulley in the tower over his head and he watched the barge lift and dip in the slight swells. It was clear that something was happening, but the barge didn't seem to be getting any closer.

"'Scuse me," Peter said to the squat teamster sitting in the driver's seat of the freighter. "That boat is coming in, isn't it?"

The teamster looked out at the barge, then down at Peter, then back out at the barge, measuring it with his eye, and then back down at Peter. He considered carefully. Then he leaned away and spat out the far side of his wagon. Then he leaned back. "Yup," he said.

"How long does it take," Peter asked, "to cross, I mean?"

The teamster considered. "You in a hurry?" he asked finally. He didn't appear to have a high regard for people in a hurry.

"No," Peter assured him. "Not really. I just wondered."

"Five trips a day," the teamster said. "Back and forth, you know. Takes all day. Dawn to dusk. Four trips in winter, five in summer. Days are shorter in winter. Not so much commerce nowadays." He scratched intently under his leather vest.

A woman emerged from a shack by the winch and walked over to Mordecai, who still sat on the wagon. She was large, heavy, and dressed in half an acre of clean denim, and she carried a ledger under her arm. "Morning," she said. "Planning to cross?"

"I had some such thought," Mordecai admitted.

She flipped open the ledger. "Name," she said, "and point of origin."

"What for?" Mordecai asked.

"Why not?" the woman replied. "You got something to hide?"

"No," Mordecai said. "I just get curious whenever anyone wants to know my business."

"It's the government," the woman explained. "Personal, I don't give a Russian damn; but we got to pay a head tax on every person and every vehicle what we take across. So the government makes us keep a record so they can check up on us. Personal, I don't care what you put down."

"I understand, my good lady," Mordecai said. "Hand me up the notebook and I shall fill it out."

The woman, who had clearly not been anyone's good lady in quite some time, handed up the ledger with a slightly glazed look in her eye. Mordecai did a bit of creative writing in the appropriate space and then handed it back.

"You have to pay now," the woman told him.

"Certainly, my good lady. What is the tariff?"

"One dollar for the wagon, ten cents a head for the passengers. That's in Washington dollars. Ten cents more on the dollar for Duchy paper; twenty-five cents more on the dollar for Los Angeles paper. Other money according, and you'd have to wait for my husband to come back and price it. No other paper, of course, nohow."

"Very clear. We'll pay in Duchy paper." Mordecai brought out a small wallet.

"I can give you a commute book if you want," the woman told him. "Twenty cents on the dollar, discounted. You only have to make ten trips a year to get the rate."

"Thank you," Mordecai said, "but I'm afraid that would be useless to us." He counted the bills into her hand and returned his wallet to the inner pocket whence it had come.

Twenty minutes later the ferry was in. Two men jumped off and tied the craft to its moorings, then pulled a ramp over from the shore to the barge. A closed coach and a flatbed wagon pulled off the ferry and headed up the dirt road to the superhighway.

The teamster pulled his wagon onto the barge and Mordecai

pulled up alongside him. The two bargemen wrapped ropes around the wheels of the wagons and tied them down to the sides of the barge.

The trip across took slightly over an hour. Mordecai spent the time studying an old road map printed by a long-defunct oil company, making notations and drawing conclusions. Peter and Ruth sat at the edge of the barge and dangled their feet into the water. They held hands and talked about the meaning of life, and other important things that young lovers discuss.

When they had reached the other shore and the wagon was on the highway again, Peter and Ruth climbed over to join Mordecai in the driver's seat. "We'd like to talk to you," Peter said.

Mordecai chuckled. "I'm not going anywhere," he said. "Except east. For the next three thousand miles I am your captive audience, and you are mine. At five miles an hour, average, when we're moving."

"That's kind of what we want to discuss," Ruth said. "What's the point of this? I mean, the trip."

"How much hope have we got of accomplishing anything?" Peter added. "Are we going to do any good?"

"I'm not a seer," Mordecai told them. "I cannot prophesy, although I'm pretty good at explaining. Is this what you two were looking so serious about while we were on that barge? Incidentally, I thought you'd been warned about public displays of affection. No more hand-holding in front of the savages; it provokes them. Could the bargemen or the teamster hear you discuss the imminent doom of the human race?"

"I don't think so," Peter said.

"No," Ruth said, "I was checking."

"Good girl."

"That doesn't answer the question," Peter said stubbornly. "We're not asking you to predict the future, just to make an educated guess."

"You want me to assure you that your life will be worthwhile? No one can do that. Your life will be what you make it."

"In twenty years or less we might all be dead," Peter said. "What's worthwhile then?"

"In a hundred years you will most assuredly be dead. Why bother doing anything?"

Peter shook his head. "It's not the same thing. I'm talking about the possible death of everyone. Everyone."

"Peter," Mordecai said, "consider: In a hundred and fifty years or so everyone now alive will be gone, and a new generation will have taken over. Or, perhaps, it won't. In neither case will the result interest you."

"Are you saying that we shouldn't try to do anything because it's not worthwhile?" Peter asked. "If so, what are we—you—doing here?"

"That's not what I'm saying," Mordecai said. "If I'd wanted to say that, I would have. Tell me: If I said that I thought we could do no good, that it was all wishful thinking; that the Martian was probably going to die in orbit because the shuttle won't leave the space station, and even if he does get down the vaccine won't work; and in any case there's no way on Earth for us to produce and distribute the vaccine in useful quantities, so that even if we do save a number of people it's back to savagery, back all the way to the cave, because there won't be enough people alive to retain a culture; and that unless immunity is passed by the mother's bloodstream, the next generation will never be born because there's no way in hell for a bunch of savages to manufacture the serum. Did you follow all that? Good! Tell me, if I were to say that—if I truly believed that—then what? Would you go home?"

"No, of course not," Ruth said.

"That's not the point!" Peter insisted.

"On the contrary," Mordecai said. "That's exactly the point. We've got a job to do. We're to wander across the continent distributing little booklets and boxes of samples in the hope that they will help save the human race. When we reach the East Coast we're going to deliver a load of microfiched books and various artifacts in the hope that someday someone will be able to glean one useful fact from the mass of data. If that's worth doing, we'll do it, and we'll do it the best we can. If it's not worth doing, let's go back to the bay and I'll spend the rest of my life fishing. It's up to you."

"Why?" Peter asked.

"I like fishing."

"It's worth doing," Ruth said. "Of course it is."

"Yes? Now: Is it worth doing *whether or not we succeed?*"

"Yes, it is."

"Good! Then my answer to you is: I don't know. I don't know if we'll succeed; I don't know if it will do any good; I don't know if the human race will survive. But we are doing good. We're doing the best we can, and that's good."

Peter frowned. "Aren't you laying it on a little heavy?"

Mordecai shrugged. "Try me on 'what is life?' sometime."

They jogged on in silence. That evening they settled down to sleep under walnut trees somewhere east of Vacaville. They were very alone. The population density was low in the Central Valley, and people had a tendency to cluster together since the Death. The three-hundred-year-old tradition of the American farmer who lived on the land he farmed was now obsolete. The European system of farmers living in a town and going out every morning to tend their land had taken its place. The farmers banded together for mutual protection after the Death—in the years when any stranger, no matter how harmless or potentially useful, might be a threat, bringing the Death with him.

By early the next afternoon the wagon had reached the outskirts of Sacramento. For some reason the highway, now Interstate 80, deteriorated rapidly as it approached the city. There were broad cracks through the concrete, in which grew a variety of healthy grasses, plants, and an occasional young tree. Ahead of the wagon, lizards basked by the side of the cracks but they darted underground at the approaching hoofbeats.

Then, as the outskirts became suburbs and then city, the road improved again. There were a good number of wagons and coaches, of a variety of styles and a range of workmanship, on the road. Many of them included bits of automobile in their construction: here a fender, there a windshield, a rear door with roll-down windows in the side of a one-horse van, a sedan roof suspended by wooden pillars over a boxy-looking carriage. The breed of automobile might now be extinct, but the carapaces of these long-dead monsters still littered the countryside; and man, like the hermit crab, was not averse to using the empty shells for purposes of his own.

The bridge across the Sacramento River was still standing, but the city on the other side was well on the way to becoming one with Nineva and Tyre. A large section of it to the north had burned to the ground, presenting a vast chessboard of cement-gray lines forming brown and green squares with an occasional blackened rook of a burned-out building squatting in place. The southern section, spared the fire, was merely rotting and collapsing in on itself.

They crossed the bridge and proceeded down route 80 along the divider between rot and burn. The traffic was heavier than they had seen before, most of it going in their direction. Along the side of the road, spaced well apart, were a series of produce wagons with their sides down and outside awnings up. They ranged from bright colors to bare wood and canvas; from one small wagon alone to a pride of three large ones grouped in a U with umbrella-covered tables in the middle. Hand-painted signs identified their products. PORCPY said the sign above one, with an illustrative picture painted below. HOTT DOG & BUN & BEER read a second, with a picture that could have been a snake attacking a fire hydrant, but was probably a hot dog and a mug. A third, with a picture that could have been anything, said ROST CORN. "As these people get more illiterate," Mordecai said, waving at the sign, "they're going to have to learn to paint a lot more realistically than that."

"Maybe it has already become stylized," Ruth suggested. "Maybe that symbol means 'corn' to everyone in the Central Valley, and the Latin letters are only for illiterate clods like us."

Peter climbed up from inside the wagon. "What's happening?" he asked.

"We have found civilization, such as it is," Mordecai told him. "The restaurant, I believe, is the mark of the civilized man."

Peter looked around and shrugged. "Why?" he asked. "Why all the wagons, and where's everyone going?"

Mordecai pointed straight ahead to where the road twisted, divided, and cloverleafed. A large banner was hanging from the overpass. "Can you read that?" he asked. "It should tell us."

Peter peered. "No."

"Well then, patience," Mordecai counseled. "Another minute or two and we should have the answer."

A small wagon, even smaller than their own, pulled up alongside them and the driver, a lad just coming out of acne, leaned toward them. "Say!" he shouted in a confidential manner, "that's quite a handsome wagon you folk have there. And them rubber wheels; where'd you get them rubber wheels?"

"Found 'em in a can," Mordecai yelled back.

The boy nodded wisely. Everyone knew that the best things came in a can. "Lucky," he called. "What you selling?"

"What's that?" Mordecai asked.

"What you selling? Or are you displaying or fabricating or entertaining? Why are you going to the fair? Say, you're not jugglers, are you? Had some jugglers here two years ago. I like jugglers. Practiced myself for months, but I never could get past two lemons. There must be some trick to it."

"Look me up at the fair," Mordecai yelled across to him, "I'll show you."

"You a juggler?"

"Not a very good one," Mordecai said.

"Oh," the boy said, with the air of one who has learned to put up with life's disappointments. "Anyrate, see you there." He pulled up ahead of them.

The banner, now that they were close enough to read it, read MIDSUMMER'S FAIR. There was no illustration below except an arrow pointing to the left. They, like most of the traffic, followed the arrow.

There was another bridge, over a stream called the American River, and there, ahead of them, lay the fairground. On the left was a concrete parking lot, with wagons and carriages packed in close order. Past the lot was a great grassy plain with several two-story, glass-and-concrete Golden Age buildings widely disbursed and a network of garish tents, wagons, corrals, and stockades forming the streets, alleys, squares, plazas, and playgrounds of this wood-and-canvas temporary city.

"What do we do?" Peter asked as they approached the crystalline confusion of the fair.

"Join in," Mordecai told him. "A perfect opportunity to test our cover."

"Which cover?" Ruth asked. They had prepared several acts to use depending on the intellectual and critical climate of the audience.

Mordecai wet his finger and held it up to the air. "Magic!" he said. "These people don't have the feel of the sort of audience who would burn prestidigitators at the stake. We shall do a few small illusions for them. Shake the moths out of Messrs. Waggoner and Johnson's apparatus. Saw a young lady in half, perhaps."

"Thrilling," Ruth said.

〜〜〜〜〜〜

The *Odysseus* was returning home. Three hundred twenty-two light seconds out from Mars, over a month to go before rendezvous with *Quetzalcoatl*, the space station waiting in orbit around the Earth; waiting for seventy-three years.

Speed: 7.7 kilometers per second relative to Earth, and increasing constantly as the laws of celestial mechanics brought it into Earth orbit.

Pilot: Socrates Proudfoot. Thirty-four years old (Earth), and the pick of the volunteers. One hundred seventy centimeters tall, sixty-one kilos, hair brown, eyes brown, with a steady gaze that focused somewhere through you when he looked at you, and left you with the feeling that he knew, and understood. It was a trick of the eyes that has been noticed among some men who take responsibility for the lives of others. Nelson, it is said, had it in his one eye; Lincoln had it, and Clair Chennault. Some bomber pilots and submarine commanders during World War II developed it. It had been common in space. It was not unusual on Mars.

Cargo: twenty-three vials of living virus; deep-frozen for their trip through space, but that doesn't kill a virus.

Socrates thought a lot about the many things that could still go wrong; the many ways in which he could still be instantly killed, or slowly and impotently die in orbit around Earth, leaving the virus to remain frozen until someday it and he warmed and then boiled and then vaporized in a great meteor splash across Earth's atmosphere.

Socrates thought, but he did not worry: he planned. He anticipated. He practiced. He drew alternate answers from the ship's computer and studied them and made them a part of his reflexes. Mars had chosen well.

~~~~~~~~~

Getting a place in the fairground was no problem, although the procedure defied all logic. Peter did the preliminary scouting. "Go see the fair director," he was told.

"Who is the fair director," he asked, "and where do I find him?"

"The who?"

"The fair director?"

"Ain't no one 'round here by that title. What you want to see him about, anyway?"

The trouble was, he couldn't get a continuous answer out of any one person. Everyone was too hurried to do more than listen to his question in passing and shout out an answer over his shoulder as he scurried by. "The fair director!" Peter shouted to a broad-shouldered gentleman who was passing with a twenty-foot tree on his back.

"Sure do, don't they?" the gentleman agreed as he staggered by.

Finally Peter found a small, self-assured man sitting by a large tent pole, smoking a pipe; an island of human tranquility amid a sea of endeavor. "Pardon me," Peter said, removing his busby, "but I'm looking for the fair director."

The little man squinted up at Peter and then at the sun. "For the next two hours or so, that's me," he said. "Then the sun goes down and I eat dinner. Tomorrow morning this place opens to the public. Although, judging by your costume, you ain't no public; ain't it?"

Peter unbuttoned the top few buttons on his cossack's jacket and admitted to the truth of this.

"You ain't selling charms or spells or the like, are you? 'Cause I warn you right now, I don't give a damn if it rains or it don't.

Anything up to a typhoon, I figure, would only break the monotony."

"No spells," Peter assured him. "I want a location assigned to my wagon."

"Now that's different. What you do? What category? Selling? Fixing? Making? Showing? Growing? Faking? Different rates for different fates. What's yours?"

"We, ah, sell medicine," Peter said.

"I see," the man said, sucking on his pipe. "Entertainment. That's Madam Bonecia. Cost you twenty per cent of your gross. You agreeable? That means twenty cents on the dollar."

"Sounds fair," Peter agreed, wondering if it did.

"Very good. Go see Madam Bonecia; she'll doss you."

"Where is she?" Peter asked. He wanted to add, "and what is 'doss'?" but was afraid of sounding stupid.

"The mitt tent over there," the man said, waving a hand in the general direction of his rear.

"Right," Peter said. "Where?"

The man pointed again. "Small tent," he said, "big sign. Picture of a palm divided up by black lines."

"Right," Peter said. "Thank you." He went off.

Madam Bonecia was a gross woman in a red-checked dress and an expanse of white apron. She sat cross-legged—or Peter assumed she was cross-legged, since her legs were invisible under the wide folds of her dress; perhaps she hadn't any legs at all—in the middle of her tent, taking up most of the available space. "Yes, dearie," she called to Peter when he paused outside. "Come right on in!"

"Madam Bonecia?"

"In the," she giggled, "flesh. What can I do for you? You don't want your palm read? I thought not. Youth is so seldom inquisitive about the future, it has so much of it coming."

"The fair director sent me over," Peter told her. "He said you'd doss us."

"You in the grift?" the woman asked in some surprise. "What's your calling?"

"We sell medicine," he said, hoping he had understood the question properly.

"I'll be damned," Madam Bonecia said. "They get younger every day. Welcome to the Midsummer Fair, youth. What is your name?

Peter? Good name. Call me Marcia; everyone does. Well, that's
not strictly true; I am called other things. But you wouldn't use
language like that, would you?" She produced a rolled chart from
a fold in the tent and pinned the outside corners to the rug with
cork-handled pins. Unrolling the chart, she then pinned down the
other two corners. "Where, oh where," she murmured, staring at
the profusion of colored lines, squiggles, squares, dots, blotches,
smudges, and smears in front of her, "where will it all end? What
does any of this mean? You're not expected to answer any of these
questions, you know. They're purely rhetorical. Ah, here's a good
place for you, I think. The question is: Is it still free—unencum-
bered—untrammeled—empty—stark—virgin—so to speak, available? These fucking maps are way out of date. Way! It must be
two hours since corrections have been brought around. Two hours.
And you know what can happen in two hours? You know?"

She seemed to be waiting for Peter to answer, but he wasn't
sure what the question was. "Excuse me?" he said, hoping she
wouldn't be offended at his inability to follow her conversation.

"Certainly," she told him. "Excused. Try this spot first." She
tapped a rust-colored area of the chart with a skinny stiletto which
appeared in her hand. "If it's been taken, come back and I'll place
you somewhere else. The corrections should be in by then. It's
perfectly idiotic, you know, this system of letting the different
guilds or professions space their own people and then running
around to find out who has put whom where. Idiotic. Go get settled now."

"Thank you," Peter said. "That area on the map—where is it?"

"Come in through the midway to shin alley, up past the blacksmith's, and you can set your wagon on the right, between a—I
believe—potter, or plater, or platterer, or some such; and a candle-
maker. If you can't find it, ask for the blacksmith's. Every stud
with a horse knows where he is by this time."

"Thank you, Madam Bonecia," Peter said, backing out of her
tent and closing the flap.

"Marcia!" she called out after him. "And open that thing—it's
hotter than a lactating virgin in here!"

Peter refastened the flap and ran off. He arrived back at the
wagon out of breath, to be rewarded by the sight of Ruth in her
"Seductive Innocence" costume: a simple white gown that covered

demurely from neck to toes, while clinging provocatively to breast and hip, outlining in shadow the shape concealed beneath. "Well," he said, stopping to admire, "that's the best view of you I've had since we left Palisades."

Ruth laughed and jumped off the wagon to join him. "Is love-making in the dark so unrewarding for you? I believe primitive people made that part of the ritual."

Mordecai's head suddenly appeared from beneath a wagon flap. "These primitive people around here don't want to hear about it either," he whispered hoarsely. "If you get into trouble because of your hot, passionate natures again; this time I never heard of either of you."

Peter blew Ruth a silent kiss and climbed up to take the reins. He piloted the wagon to its proper location across from the black-smith's outdoor display of ironmongery and muscles without a mistake and with only a few minor hesitations. Then he and Mordecai set about setting up the small platform stage, while Ruth, with a robe on over her costume, took their three horses back to the entertainers' corral and negotiated with the hostler for their feed and care.

When the stage was set and they were busy stringing up the sedate red-and-white bunting around the canvas top, a small man in nattily tailored formal dress, which looked to be made out of some rough-weave fabric and dyed a variety of shades of black, stood in front of the stage and watched Peter and Mordecai climb around as though that were the show. They paused on impulse and stared back at him. He tipped his hat. "Greetings," he said. "Welcome to the fair, fellow citizens. Madam Bonecia sent me over to fetch you. I am Dr. Fleece. 'My name is known from sea to sea, and all the spirits converse with me; so if you would contact a shade, I'll put you through once I am paid.' My motto. There are several other verses. I don't believe I know either of you two gentlemen. New to the grift?"

"We have, ah, been working in other parts of the land," Mordecai said. "I am the Great Mordecai, and this is my assistant, Peter."

"Howdja do? Come on over when you're set up. We're laying out the grub. You could bring a bottle of the old and cold, if you're so inclined."

"There's a young lady with us," Mordecai said.

"Course there is. What kind of grift without a frail? See you there." With a smile and a wave he trotted off.

"I had thought," Mordecai remarked thoughtfully to Peter, while staring at the retreating back, "that we were entering a currently unexploited field. Reinstituting an old American custom. But apparently I was mistaken. The grift seems to be alive and flourishing."

"The grift?" Peter asked. "That's what she called it. Madam Bonecia. What does it mean?"

"So they haven't even changed the cant in the past hundred years," Mordecai said. "I read a few old books and thought I was probably the world's only living expert on a dead art—art?—and here I find it alive and bitching. A grift is a scam by which a mechanic separates a mark from his poke by showing him the glim."

"Do that again," Peter demanded.

"A grift is a method of removing the loose cash from a man by giving him, or promising him, something that he thinks is of great value, which usually turns out to be worthless, or unavailable. 'The grift' is the loose brotherhood of people in this profession."

"I see," Peter said. "Isn't that of, ah, questionable morality?"

"Yes," Mordecai said.

When Ruth returned Mordecai produced a jug of hard cider from within the van and they went off to dine with their confreres.

The men and women gathered in Madam Bonecia's tent were a colorful and flamboyant group. Aside from this common tendency toward extroversion, they were as diverse an assemblage as could be brought under one roof. Madam Bonecia had removed the back wall of the area Peter had first met her in, thus opening up the whole back area of the tent and tripling the available room. The guests still filled up all available space. They all seemed to want to talk at once, and would fight to lead the conversation. But despite this tendency, when one of them succeeded in getting the floor the rest of them listened devoutly. There was a small, intense girl who wandered about the tent grabbing people by the elbow, looking up into their eyes, and making pronouncements. When she got to Peter she said: "I sense some deep inner conflict in your soul."

"Of what sort?" Peter asked, but she had already moved on.

At Mordecai's side she stared up into his eyes and announced: "I wish I had your wisdom."

"I wish I had your body," Mordecai told her, but she had released his elbow and glided away.

"What is it, exactly, that you pitch?" a very tall man with a pointed beard asked Mordecai.

"I probe the innermost secrets of the human mind," Mordecai told him.

"A mentalist," the man said, satisfied. "Swell. I probe the top of the head, meself."

"Your meaning, sir, eludes me," Mordecai said.

"Really," the man chuckled. "Fancy that! And not even one of my innermost secrets. Allow me to introduce meself: Dr. Mirable, the world's foremost authority on the ancient science of phrenology."

"Ah!" Mordecai said. "How nice." He pumped Dr. Mirable's hand. "A student of the bump. My pleasure, sir."

Dinner was a giant pot of stew served in earthenware bowls and accompanied by a type of flat, round bread that Peter and Ruth were unfamiliar with. A giant mound of boiled corn sat by the side of the stewpot on a wooden plank. The conversation ranged from esoteric aspects of showmanship to how to clean bloodstains off a broadloom rug. Much of the discussion was on the towns and territories of divided America: how they were governed, how they were policed, what the prevalent ethos, philosophy, religion, business attitude, mythos, and superstitions were; and how all this would affect the fraternity of grifters.

"Now the Duchy," Dr. Mirable said, "that's prime territory all over. Course you got to watch out for the sensibilities in some towns. Got rid of all books but the Bible, some of them have. And a few of them use stranger Bibles than Gideon ever dreamed of."

"Gideon?"

"He's a gent what used to go around planting Bibles the way Johnny spread appleseeds. Don't know whether he's myth or man, but that's the story. If you wander about much in the US of A, or in the Southern Confederacy, you'll run across Gideons with their packs of Bibles across their backs strutting up and down the countryside."

"Ever been down by the Los Angeles Freecity?" a lively little man called Dennis the Gent asked. He took off the top hat that was his trademark and held it in front of his chest. "Now *that's* weirdland, if you know what I mean. Down by the bay the Free Scientists of Religious Gospel have about a square mile marked off to themselves. They believe in the Active Nonexistence of God and the Sublimity of Matter. And if you want to work that area— hell, if you want to pass through with all your teeth—you goddamn well better believe it too, if you know what I mean."

"What does all that stuff mean?" Madam Bonecia asked from her raised, thronelike canvas chair at the back of the tent.

"Beats me," Dennis the Gent told her. "But if you're willing to swear you believe it when they ask, they don't bother much trying to explain it to you. Then, over in Santa Monica, they got the Constructive Agnostics of the One God."

"I thought agnostics didn't believe in God," Madam Bonecia said.

"I think they don't know," Peter volunteered.

Dr. Mirable chuckled. "They don't know," he said, "but they *know* that they don't know."

"This bunch isn't concerned with that," Dennis the Gent explained. "The question is, as far as they're concerned, whether God believes in them. You know, it's very disconcerting to have someone come poke his nose in your face and yell, 'Brother, does God believe in you?' They take it very personally. There's always a couple of them rolling about on the ground feeling the strength of God's belief in them. They listen in tongues.

"Then there's the Scientographers over in old L.A. It's hard to tell just what they do believe, but they sure talk pretty. They can range over all of known space and time, from one end of the universe to the other and from the time of dinosaurs to the heat-death of the sun, with the aid of this little gadget of theirs. It's a kind of a top at the end of a piece of string that you hold over someone's open palm. It either goes in a circle or straight back and forth, and that's very significant. They carry them around all the time and test each other with them."

"They travel back and forth through time?" Mordecai asked, interested.

"That's what they say. That is, if that's what they're saying— it's kind of hard to tell, if you know what I mean."

"Then there's the enclaves," Dr. Mirable offered. "What do you
think they believe?"

"They seem to believe pretty much in keeping to themselves,"
Dennis the Gent said. "Very, I calls it, antisocial, if you know what
I mean."

"What do you mean?" Mordecai asked. "Don't they let you in?"

"Oh, sure, good for a night's doss, if you're willing to help a bit
with the dishes, and maybe a few magic tricks for the kids; but no
chance to make an honest living, if you know what I mean. No
grifting allowed, and very peculiarly strict and self-righteous about
it they are."

"What's your grift?" Dr. Mirable asked.

"You never heard of the Gent's Patent Potion? Good for all
that ails you. Puts weight on the skinny, takes fat off the fat; if
you're bald, just rub it on your head for two weeks; if you've got
a toothache, swizzle it around inside your mouth four times a day
for a week, and maybe you won't have to pull the tooth.

"How does it work, you ask me; under what principle does this
miraculous cure-all achieve its almost-unbelievable effects? You
would ask that, would you? Well, I will answer you. I tell you, la-
dies and gentlemen, that this bottle"—by now Dennis the Gent
was up on a chair and waving the bottle of green liquid over his
head—"and the miraculous elixir that it contains will cure any
human ill. Low back pains from stooping over? Take a spoonful
before bedtime. Constipation? Take two spoonsful upon arising.
Diarrhea? Take a spoonful before each meal. That's how it works,
folks; and I have the testimonials to prove it!"

Dennis the Gent received a good round of applause as he
stepped off the chair. His place was immediately taken by a large
man with a round face who extolled the virtues of two large metal
plates that were strapped to opposite sides of the body to encourage the "Psychic Flow That is so Essential to the Maintenance
of the Proper Balance of Bodily Fluids."

As the night went on one guest followed another on the chair-
stage, and their spiels arced past hyperbole into morbid fantasy.
They were spieling to their friends what they'd always wanted to
spiel to the marks when the sun was high and the wine was corked.

"Why, sir, the past and future are as opened books to me, which
I peruse at will; and on this page I find . . . you. Your past? You

were born in excrement like a fly; but, unlike a fly, you haven't the
sense or the wings to remove yourself. And from that viewpoint,
nose-level with the ordure, you impose your views, your ethics, and
your morality on all who come within your ken. Your present?
You are alive; no more, no less. You don't know why, it has never
occurred to you to ask. You live for the food you eat and the
women you lay and the occasional flashes of joy you get when you
strike down and destroy something you do not understand. Your
future? You will not be."

The common factor that Peter saw in the personalities of these
showmen was a cynicism bordering on hate toward the mark—the
outsider.

"I hope I never get like that," he said to Mordecai when they
were back in the tent they had set up. "These people don't like or
trust anybody who isn't in the grift."

"Like everyone else," Mordecai said, shrugging. "There are no
cosmopolitans anymore."

"But these people spend their lives traveling around and meeting people—"

"Yes," Mordecai agreed. "And getting spit on and chased out
of towns and arrested—where they still perform that service—and
worse. They have no reason to like the marks."

"It's because they cheat them," Ruth said. "If you're going to
cheat someone you can't have any respect for him. Clearly."

"Clearly," Mordecai agreed. "We, of course, love everybody because of our great understanding and empathy. Now go to sleep—
or something." He rolled himself in his bedroll and put his face
to the canvas and spoke no more that night.

~~~~~~~~~

13

They stayed at the fair for three days. In the afternoon of the second day Mordecai sent Ruth to the small enclave that had once been Sacramento State, with a small bundle of booklets and apparatus. The dean of the enclave told her that they were mostly concerned with growing green vegetables and remaining literate, but they would do what they could.

By the evening of the third day Peter and Ruth were getting over their stagefright and beginning to enjoy their parts in the show. Mordecai found it necessary to remind them that, with the bundle delivered, the only excuse for remaining was to practice their act. Now that they felt secure in it, it was time to go.

Their compatriots were sorry to see them go and obviously curious as to why they would leave while the fair had a few days to run, but too polite to ask.

They assembled their gear and left the fairground at dusk of the third day. They didn't plan to go far in the dark, but dusk was the only time they could get their wagon off the grounds. Even then it was a slow, aggravating process and it was quite dark by the time they were out. They tied up east of the fairground and slept in the wagon.

The next morning Madam Bonecia sent one of the fair's gophers over to invite them back for breakfast. The lad agreed to stay and watch the wagon, so they walked the quarter mile back to the fair. The whole troupe was at the breakfast, and each person found a chance to come over and deliver a parting word of advice. "You didn't give us a chance to have a dinner for you last night," Madam Bonecia told them, " 'cause you didn't tell us you was leaving until too late. So we're having a breakfast. Have to be short, though. Got to set up before the rubes start wandering around."

"Good-bye to you," Dr. Mirable said, pumping Mordecai's hand. "Good luck, wherever you're headed. If you need anything, just mention my name anywhere west of the US of A. Hope we work together again real soon. You're good people."

After breakfast they headed back to the wagon. "Boy," Peter said, "if they accept you, they really go all out."

Mordecai belched.

They hitched up the horses and moved out. In a short time they were in rolling foothills with mountains beyond. By the next day they were in the mountains, and for days after that they were in the mountains. Their distance per day was cut to one third or less by the slopes. Downhill time was no better than uphill time, and going down a steep slope was much more hair-raising than going up the other side. Going uphill the horses pulled, and one of the humans rode the brakes, putting them on to relieve the strain whenever a horse stumbled or faltered. Going down the horses and brakes both worked continually to prevent any momentum building up. There were four brakes, one leather pressure pad for each wheel rim, which could be worked separately or together. During steep grades the back brakes were kept on continually, wearing out a pair of the leather pads about every two miles.

For five days they didn't pass another human being on the road. Then, on the morning of the sixth day, a great covered wagon pulled by six oxen crested the hill in front of them. When it reached them the driver pulled his team to a stop and Mordecai did likewise.

"Oatman!" Mordecai said, extending his hand across the gap.

"Mordecai!" the driver said, solemnly shaking his hand with extreme economy of motion. "What are you doing out here? Not satisfied with my service?" A neatly printed sign painted black across the white canvas of the wagon said: OATMANS ROCKY MOUNTAIN UP AND DOWN EXPRESS. Oatman himself was a short, stocky man with no evidence of hair anywhere about his head.

"Taking a little trip," Mordecai told him. "Expanding my horizons, as it were. Peter, Ruth, meet my old friend and wholesaler, Oatman."

Ruth nodded politely. Peter jumped down and ducked under

the shaft, coming up between the two wagons. "A pleasure to meet you, sir."

"Well!" Oatman said, beaming across to Mordecai. "Real polite one, isn't he?" He waved a thumb toward the interior of his wagon. "My two helpers are asleep at the moment. Which is usually a safe statement, with those two."

"What's happening in the great eastern world?" Mordecai asked. "Anything new? Anything worth knowing?"

"Depends 'pon how far you're going," Oatman said, reaching into a leather bucket by his side and popping something from it into his mouth. "No trouble up through Salt Lake. Hell, there's almost no people from here to there. The Latter Day community around Salt Lake is getting bigger and more self-righteous every month, so watch your step when you get there."

"Religious trouble?" Mordecai asked.

"No, not at all. They're all good, honest, hard-working, God-fearing, clean-living people, and you'd damn well better be the same." His hand made another excursion from bucket to mouth. "It's probably a good idea to be afraid of the same god they're afraid of, but you can safely quake in a different way. But you'd better work at something, and it better be something they consider work. No hobos or backpackers welcome. And keep away from Salt Lake City."

"Why is that?"

"Most of the downtown area is taboo. Only the faithful are allowed to enter this holy of holies."

"What happens if you try?" Peter asked out of curiosity. "The ghosts scare you off?"

"They shoot you, most like," Oatman said, popping another something into his mouth. "Very pragmatic people."

"And further east?" Mordecai asked.

"You planning to go further east?" Oatman sounded surprised. "You're okay until Nebraska Free State—somewhere around there." He noticed Peter staring at his hand as it came from the bucket and opened his fist, holding it down to Peter. "Cracked corn," he explained. "Good to munch on, if you've got teeth. Want some?"

"Thank you." Peter took a handful of the dry, multicolor kernels and contemplated them.

"What's happening in Nebraska?"

"Somewhere 'round there; hard to tell where boundaries are these days, 'cause there ain't any. The United States, all eight of 'em, is under the control of a guy called Brother Simon. He's some kind of nut. Trying to consolidate the US of A territory. Every time he consolidates, it gets larger; but that's none of my concern. They leave travelers and teamsters alone for the most part. But the farmers aren't too happy about it, I hear. They don't care whether they're US of A or Free State of Nebraska, long as the taxes stay about the same. The 'claves in the area just want to be left alone, and both sides are happy to oblige."

"You mean there's fighting going on?"

"I think they call it a war," Oatman said. "People getting killed, towns getting burned. That Simon's a nut."

"But there's no trouble getting through?"

"Not if you're righteous at figuring out what's the smallest bribe a man will take and stay bought."

"Fascinating," Mordecai said. "There is nothing new. Would you like to chock your wheels, friend Oatman, and join us for lunch —or dinner—or whatever you call the midday meal? And your two assistants, of course."

"Admire to, Mordecai. Course we'll chip in to the pot. If the little lady can cook—"

"Just because I'm a woman," Ruth bristled, "is no reason to assume I'm the cook for this menage. Women are good for other things, you know."

"No offense," Oatman said, looking as shocked as if one of his kernels had just bitten him back. "Unwarranted assumption, don't know why I made it. As many ways of doing things as there are towns on this continent. I certainly don't care who cooks the meal you're inviting me to share—if I'm still invited—I assure you. Cook it myself, for that matter. Sorry."

"I'm sorry," Ruth said. "I shouldn't have snapped. Practically the first words I spoke to you, too."

Mordecai slowly lowered himself out of the driver's seat and climbed down to the road. "Making you perform more than your fair share of the culinary exercises, are we?" he asked Ruth. "That could well be. We shall remedy that. Equality in every way, that's my motto. As long as you maintain a proper reverence for your elders."

It was just before dusk that evening when they came to their first ghost city. Oatman had mentioned to them that they were close to Reno, and there it was before them, rising like a wart on the face of the desert plateau. The glass that was left in the buildings glittered multicolor with the backlighting of the setting sun: little specks of gemstone in the basalt. It was particularly impressive as there was nothing gradual about it: the city began abruptly on all sides, as though it had been picked up from somewhere else and set in place. They reached it shortly after sunset and camped on the outskirts just before the dark came down like thunder.

~~~~~~~~~~

14

"Cadet Wail!"

"Yes, sir?"

"Do you know why you're here?"

"No, sir." Wail had a clear conscience. To the best of his recollection, and he had been recollecting in depth for the past half hour since told to report to the discipline officer, he had done nothing worthy of notice for the past few days.

"Amazing," Captain Spaulding commented. "The cadet grapevine isn't as efficient as it was when I was a lad. You are unaware, then, that we conducted a surprise inspection of all lockers this afternoon?"

"Oh," Wail said. "No, sir. I mean, yes, sir. I mean, I am aware of it, sir." He stood at strict attention and stared at the top of Captain Spaulding's bald head five feet away from him across the clean expanse of metal desk top. Spaulding liked you to stand at strict attention while you spoke to him. Spaulding was the sort of unimaginative, strict martinet who enjoyed the post of discipline officer, a post he had held for nine years.

"You knew about the inspection?"

"Yes, sir." Wail didn't add that, cadet grapevines being what they are, everyone had known about it hours before it happened. When officers ate lunch in the mess hall with the cadets they were planning something. If the officers dressed in fatigues, it was probably a surprise field exercise. When they were in class A uniform, it was quite possibly a surprise inspection of the men, or their lockers.

"And you don't know why you're here?"

"No, sir." It sounded like someone had planted some contraband in his locker. Wail wondered what it could be. For the first time in the interview he was beginning to feel nervous. How can you convince someone of a negative? That you're not stupid enough to leave contraband in your locker at any time? Particularly when the one you have to convince is a rigid, sadistic bully who sure as hell wants to find you guilty of something. What could it be? Tobacco? Dirty pictures? A weapon? Stolen goods? Skins? Or one of the lesser proscriptions: food, soiled clothing, civilian clothes, something like that?

Well, he was about to find out. His palms, he noted, were sticky. The fear reaction is not one that comes only upon the guilty.

Spaulding slowly pulled open the top drawer of his desk and slid his hand inside. Even more slowly he withdrew a standard green-covered, rope-bound notebook of the size used by most students and cadets at the exclave. He put the notebook on top of his desk, centering it carefully on the barren expanse of gray paint, and closed the drawer with his elbow. "Is this yours?" he asked, with a sneer in his voice.

"I have no way of knowing, sir, from the outside," Wail said, doing his best to keep the tremor out of his voice. Now he really had no idea of what was going on, and he was frightened. The sonofabitch captain was getting to him.

"No way of knowing, sir, from the outside," Spaulding mimicked in a quavering falsetto. He flipped open the notebook without looking at it. "Well?" His eyes were fastened on Wail's face.

Wail looked down at the notebook. Spaulding had opened it to a blank page. The emperor has no clothes. Wail wanted to giggle.

"Well?" Spaulding demanded.

"I'm sorry, sir, but there's nothing written on that page."

Spaulding looked down, very irritated, and riffled through the pages until he came to one which had writing on it. "You write that?" he asked, turning the book until the angular handwriting faced Wail.

"Yes, sir."

"Read it!"

"Excuse me?"

"What?"

"Sir. Excuse me, sir."

"Read it. Aloud."

"Yes, sir." It was a poem. Wail wasn't particularly proud of it, but he doubted whether Captain Spaulding was esthetically competent to judge anybody's poetry, even his. So he read:

"THOUGHTS ON GUARD DUTY AT 3 A.M.
In the cavern, row on row, is
Piece on piece of apparatus
Dormant in the coming darkness
All that's left of corporate business
All we know of who begat us
Row on row they squat and listen
For the sound of the returning
Of their long-gone operators
In the candlelight they glisten
Burnished for the coming darkness
We who keep the candles burning
In the early morning hours
Hear the sounds of the creators
Fear the sounds of the creators
Coming for their waiting children
Do they come for flesh-and-blood kin
Or for plastic, glass, and iron?"

Wail put down the notebook and resumed the position of attention. Captain Spaulding stared at him while he stared at the wall. Neither of them said anything for a time.

Captain Spaulding broke the silence. "Well?"

"I guess," Wail said, "it's not very good."

"Not very good?" Spaulding yelped as though something had stung him on the "good." "Is that the point? Is that all you can think of to say? Is that what I called you in here for, to make critical judgments on this tripe?"

"I don't know, sir," Wail admitted.

"Do you think we're all ignoramuses here?" Spaulding demanded.

Wail gulped. That was exactly what he thought. "No, sir," he insisted.

"Or what about this one?" Spaulding said, spinning the notebook around and thumbing through to another page. He read:

"TO MY ANCESTOR

ON THE JOYS OF A SURPLUS ECONOMY
You used it and
At time's first touch
You threw it out.

"I understand, but
You left so much
Of it about."

He put down the book and looked up at Wail. "Is that supposed to be funny? Humorous?" he asked.

"No, sir."

"Is it the proper function of a cadet to write poetry?" Captain Spaulding demanded, with the sneer evident in his voice.

"No, sir," Wail said. The injustice of this inquisition stoked inside of him a fury that threatened to boil out through the uniform, frozen, subservient exterior demanded of a cadet. "Poetry writing is not encouraged," he said in a dead-calm voice, "but neither is it forbidden. Sir."

Captain Spaulding picked up the notebook and weighed it in his hand as if it were a sausage. "I have no taste for poetry," he said. "I've never felt the urge to listen for the tiny wings of a butterfly, or go dancing tippy-toe among the flowers. But your, ah, preferences along that line are your own business, Cadet. I don't believe many of your classmen share your literary tastes. Perhaps that's why you find it necessary to keep the notebook hidden in the rear of your locker."

Spaulding looked up as he said this, as though it was a question and he was awaiting an answer. It was an old technique of his to provoke a revealing response. Wail remained silent.

"But this," Spaulding said, waving the book, "this I recognize. Subversion, Cadet. In this notebook I recognize subversion."

"Sir?" It was one of those vague, general, nasty words that one never expects to hear applied to oneself, like "mutiny," or "conspiracy," or "unnatural acts." Subversion: one of those nasty words in the Exclave Code of Uniform Justice, as revised, that was vague enough to cover whatever they wanted it to cover, and that was good for five to ten years in the slam.

"Subversion, Cadet: Disrespect for, and an attempt to undermine, the values and standards of the Exclave and-slash-or the Corps of Cadets. Your name is going before the committee at the next meeting on Monday. This notebook will be presented as evidence. You will appear. You have the right to, and will be expected to, bring any witnesses, documents, records, or other supportive evidence in your defense. You have no right to counsel at the committee hearing, but a stenographic record will be kept and a copy shall be provided to your counsel free of charge if you are bound over for trial on the charge. Do you understand?"

"Sir, I think that—"

"Cadet! Do you understand? Yes or no?"

"Yes. But—"

"You are dismissed. You are not under arrest, but no leaves or passes will be granted to you until this is resolved. You are to go back to your regular duty."

"Yes, sir."

"The Washington Heights guardbus leaves in ten minutes. Isn't your tour up there tonight?"

"Yes, sir."

"Then you'd better go. Dismissed."

Cadet Wail saluted, took a step backward, executed an abrupt about-face, and marched out of the room with the precision of a mechanical toy. Beneath his carefully composed features, his mind seethed with an alchemical mixture of rage, frustration, and fear. His stomach hurt.

~~~~~~~~~

15

It was impossible to skirt Salt Lake City. The road plunged on through with narrow-minded directness. Straight through the salt flats, right along the side of the Great Salt Lake, and then a dart through the concrete graveyard of the city. It was, however, possible to ignore the people encountered along the road. As long as they kept moving, it was easy. The people did most of the ignoring for them.

Having been forewarned, Mordecai and company kept moving, and kept as much as possible to the edge of the city. They had no problem.

They moved on to the plains and across the border into the Free State of Wyoming. The only sign of change from the Independent Community of the Latter Day Saints to the Free State of Wyoming was a giant sheet-metal cutout of a cowboy on a rearing bronco, waving his hat. The sign under the cowboy read:

WELCOME TO WYOMING
OBSERVE POSTED SPEED LIMITS
BUCKLE UP FOR SAFETY

Buckle what up? Peter wondered as their wagon plodded by.

This trip was proving something to Peter that he had often been told but had never believed: that you can't learn everything from books. The sum of Peter's knowledge had come from books, and much of his pleasure; and he regarded any book with the same reverence that a medieval monk would hold for a diglot palimpsest of the First Epistle of Paul the Apostle to the Corinthians. The enclaves were the old colleges and universities, and their god was knowledge. But in the old days their function was to seek out and expand knowledge, and now their task was to preserve it; and the difference was vast.

Mordecai was a better teacher than the books. Not that he tried to teach, or that Peter and Ruth sat at his feet with opened notebooks to catch his every word. Not at all. He yelled. He cursed. He demanded. He would permit any mistake once but no mistake twice. He was not an easy man to travel with. But he was usually right, and he was always fascinating.

"Something up ahead," Peter called into the wagon when they were some way into Wyoming. It was a little after midday and he was driving, while Mordecai snoozed under canvas to escape some of the prairie-summer heat and Ruth worked at getting their little radio into shape to pick up a possible Radio Chicago broadcast after dark.

Mordecai's eyes opened. "What is it?" he called, without moving.

"Dust," Peter said. "A hell of a lot of it. Something must be stirring it up."

"A dust storm?" Ruth wondered, moving up to the front of the wagon.

"I don't know anything about dust storms," Peter said, "but I would assume they need some sort of wind. There isn't a breeze, even."

Mordecai lifted his head and stared out the front flap. "I can't see a thing," he said.

"It's about a mile in front of us," Peter said. "Maybe a little more."

"A mile away," Mordecai mused, lowering his head back onto the bedroll he was using as a pillow. "Directly in front?"

"And to the right," Peter said. "And the left."

"Aha!" Mordecai said. He sat up. "The deductive processes tell me what must be in front of us. Stop the wagon."

Peter complied with the instruction, pulling the horses to a stop and setting the brake. "Mine not to reason why," he said. "Why?"

"A tornado?" Ruth guessed. "I didn't think they were so big."

Mordecai climbed over the backboard to the driver's seat. "Tornados are more precise," he said. "What you're looking at there is another sort of natural phenomenon." They looked at him expectantly while he peered off into the distance. "Hear the rumbling?" he asked.

Now that the wagon was stopped, Peter and Ruth could make out a faint rumble coming from the distant dust cloud.

"A thunderstorm," Ruth said, clapping her hands. "I've always wanted to see a thunderstorm. Two things we Californians are deprived of: snow and thunderstorms."

"I think I can promise you snow in a few months," Mordecai told her, "and probably thunderstorms as well. But you miss out now; that's not a storm of any sort. What you hear is the pitter-patter of feet."

Ruth and Peter stared at Mordecai, and even as they did the incessant rumbling grew louder. Ruth's eyes widened. "Bison!" she said.

"And if they're coming this way we're in trouble," Mordecai commented. "Hopefully they are merely crossing the road, and they'll have passed by in a couple of hours."

"But I thought they were almost extinct," Peter said. "It would take thousands of them to make that much dust."

"Probably tens of thousands," Mordecai said.

"But weren't they all destroyed by the buffalo hunters when they built the railroads?" Peter asked. "I remember from sixth-grade history."

"There were once fifty million of them," Mordecai said, "and by 1889 the number was down to exactly five hundred forty-one. Then they stopped killing them and put the remainder on a preserve. It was, I believe, the world's first attempt to save a vanishing species. By the time of the Death the herd had grown to twenty or thirty thousand, and had to be constantly culled to keep it down."

"You know so much about stuff like that," Ruth said. "Sometimes I wonder how old you are."

Mordecai laughed. "Ask me sometime, and I'll tell you all about Franklin Roosevelt—and Abe Lincoln. I don't remember Washington too well, I was quite young at the time."

"I wouldn't be surprised," Ruth said.

"So there are thirty thousand buffalo around now?" Peter asked, staring off at the dust.

"That was something over seventy years ago," Mordecai said.

"Take, let us say, ten thousand bison, half bulls and half cows. Say they have one calf per cow every two years, on the average, and that they live fifteen years, on the average. How many are there going to be in, let's say, seventy years? Assume they're sexually mature at age three."

"Are those the right figures?" Peter asked, impressed by Mordecai's seemingly inexhaustible fund of knowledge.

"I have no idea," Mordecai said. "If anything, they're conservative. But it doesn't account for the herds that run off the sides of cliffs because they're too stupid to stop running, or the bulls that get their horns locked fighting and die of starvation, or the wolf-culled calves; so it all balances out."

"Oh," Peter said.

"How many?" Mordecai asked again.

"I'll have to figure it out," Peter said.

"Me too," Ruth added as Mordecai's gaze shifted to her. "I think you use 'e.'"

"Well," Mordecai said, nodding his head toward the approaching dust cloud, "some fraction of the number you arrive at is in front of us now. We have to stay alert; the last thing we want is to have our wagon in the middle of a herd of bison. If they get closer than about a quarter mile, we'll have to back away at the same speed."

So they sat and watched as the dust cloud grew slowly closer. After a while the horses grew restive and Ruth climbed down to comfort them. "They must smell something strange," she said, gently rubbing the white spot between the mare's eyes.

The dust grew close enough so that the herd could be seen through it, and then individual bison wandered near them, although the defined edge of the herd stayed off. The animals were traveling almost due south, and it was just the slight hint of a westward drift that was threatening to engulf the wagon. The great beasts thumped along stolidly toward whatever vision of greener grass was driving their leader south.

A single curious bull detached himself from the herd and wandered over circuitously to inspect the wagon. When he was about a hundred yards away he stopped and lowered his head. The tiny red eyes stared at them for a while, and then he started swinging his massive head from side to side, as though trying to figure out what he was doing and why he was there. Then he turned three-quarters away from them and pretended he had no interest in them, but always being careful to keep them visible from the corner of one bloodshot eye.

"He's being casual," Peter said, chuckling softly. They were being careful to speak softly and move slowly so as not to spook the beast.

"He's trying to figure out what we are, in his terms," Mordecai said. "If he decides we're foe he'll attack at once and damn the torpedos, and if he decides we're friend he'll ignore us forever more, regardless of what we do. It's the classic example of the danger of prejudice, or prejudging. In the old buffalo-hunting days a hunter would ride along with the herd until he was completely accepted. Then he could just ride up to a bull, stick a rifle in its face, and squeeze the trigger. The rest of the bison would just stand there while their herdmates dropped."

The bull trotted off to rejoin the herd, deciding either that the humans were acceptable or that they didn't exist. And the herd kept up its slow excursion to the south and its even slower drift west. They moved the wagon back twice, about half a mile each time.

Three hours later the rear end of the vast herd came into view, and with it an unexpected sight: over a dozen men on skinny range ponies were traveling placidly behind the herd. They were dressed in rough leather, had pack rolls on the ponies' backs and unslung bows on their own. Their hair was long, tied back with leather strips, and in some cases braided. A couple of the ponies had saddles, but most had only a heavy pad tied on between them and their riders. Two of them approached the wagon and stopped a few yards off.

"Howdy," the short one on the left said, raising his open palm. His face was expressionless and his eyes were blank.

"Howdja do?" Mordecai replied. "It's a pleasure to see some more human beings on this vast plain."

There was no reply. The two men and their mounts could have been carved from mahogany.

"That's an impressive herd of buffalo you're following," Peter said. "We've been sitting here watching it pass for hours. Got any idea how many animals there are?"

"Bison," the short man intoned. "Many."

"Got any trade goods?" his partner, a tall skinny man with a large nose and a scraggly beard, asked in a flat voice.

"Well," Mordecai considered. "We're not in that line, but there are a few things we might be willing to trade; if you have anything we need."

The tall man nodded. "Fine."

The short man nodded. "Dicker."

"I'm willing to dicker," Mordecai said. "Sounds good to me."

The two men dropped their reins and swung off their ponies, then sat down cross-legged on the hard-packed earth. Their ponies remained impassively in place.

"It looks like we've fallen into some sort of a ritual," Mordecai said under his breath as he climbed over the side of the wagon. "Peter, come with me; but let me talk. Ruth, you wait here. We don't know whether their mores include women dickerers. This might be an 'everyone knows' situation."

"How's that?" Ruth asked.

"You know: 'everyone knows that dickering is men's work; you would insult us by bringing a woman into the circle. This means war!' Like that."

Mordecai went over to sit cross-legged facing the two bison boys. Peter joined him, hoping that the emotion that was causing his heart to beat faster and his hands to sweat was merely excitement and not fear.

Up close the two men lost whatever glamor they had at middle distance. Their clothing was misshapen, sweat-stained, and ripped. Their hair was thickly matted with some sort of grease that Peter could smell from where he sat. At least he thought it was the grease he smelled. It was a good thing the two men were not fond of smiling, since the teeth they had retained were black, and the gums of the tall man had receded to the point where the front tooth looked like it was suspended in mid-mouth. Peter had to fight an impulse to look away whenever the man opened his mouth.

"You have guns?" the short man asked.

"Not to trade," Mordecai said firmly.

"Powder?"

"No."

"Steel arrowheads?"

"No. Listen, wouldn't it be faster if—"

"Knives?"

Mordecai sighed. "No."

"Grain?"

"None we can spare."

"Cloth?"

"Some," Mordecai allowed.

"Nails?"

"No."

"Razor blades?"

"No."

"Axe heads?"

"No."

"Salt?"

"Yes," Mordecai said. "We can probably let you have a small keg of salt."

"Lye?"

"None."

"Soap?"

"Perhaps, but just a little," Mordecai said. Peter wondered what they'd use soap for, then realized that he was being unfair. Perhaps the reason they were so dirty was just that they didn't *have* any soap.

"Needles?"

"I think not."

"Pins?"

"No."

"Thread?"

And the tall one added, "Waxed, or plain."

"No," Mordecai said, "neither."

"Garlic?"

"No, I don't think so. I'll check."

"Pepper?"

"No."

"Coins, copper or silver?"

"None to trade."

The naming of goods continued for a while, eliciting a series of no's from Mordecai. Then there was a pause, while the two bison boys conferred. The short man then turned back to Mordecai. "Cloth, salt, soap, maybe garlic," he listed, "okay."

"What goods do you trade with?" Mordecai asked.

"Tanned hides, hung meat, some gold—dust, not coin, axle grease, hair grease, cheese."

"Buffalo-milk cheese?" Peter asked, surprised.

"Bison. Good stuff," the short man assured him.

"We could use a couple of hides," Mordecai said. "And maybe some fresh meat. And a bit of cheese."

"Hump the best part," the tall man said. "Sweet." The two of them rose as one and mounted their ponies. "We get," he said. "You assemble." They rode off in two separate and distinct clouds of dust.

Mordecai, Ruth, and Peter dug through the carefully stacked and packed supplies in the wagon to locate and extract the promised trade goods. "Those men aren't Indians, are they?" Ruth asked. "They don't talk much."

"They're more like cowboys," Peter said, "only they work in a different media."

"Bison boys," Ruth said. "It has a ring to it."

When the bison boys returned, Mordecai had carefully placed his trade goods in a line about ten yards away from the wagon, where he and his assistants sat quietly and watched.

There were about ten of them this time, and they all dismounted and carefully examined the line of goods: touching, smelling, shaking, tasting, mulling, and listening carefully to the bolt of cloth, keg of salt, and other exotic amenities from the mysterious West. When they were satisfied they backed off and went into a huddle to consult. Then they came forward and distributed their trade goods in a one-for-one relationship with Mordecai's line: three hides, carefully folded, next to the bolt of cloth; one hide and six fist-sized globes of cheese by the keg of salt; one hide by the three carefully wrapped bricks of brown soap; a hide full of salted bison hams next to the one clove of garlic Peter had located (he had found three, but they had decided to hang on to two). Then they mounted, backed off a few feet, and stood waiting.

"What do we do now?" Peter asked softly, watching the ten riders watching them.

"Either accept or reject, I would imagine. Take in the deals we approve, and leave the ones we don't."

"Do we approve?"

"Why not," Mordecai said. "Let's go out and gather the stuff in." He swung down off the wagon, with Peter and Ruth following. They began to pick up the bison boys' trade goods and bring them back to the wagon. The bison boys watched impassively and silently as the three of them made trips back and forth, picking up hides, cheese, and meat, and stored them with some semblance of order in the back of the wagon.

One of the bison boys, who looked to be much older than the rest, although it was hard to tell, urged his pony a few deliberate steps forward during the loading and peered closely at Ruth. He was a small man with hard, knotted muscles like those of the scrawny pony on whose back he was perched. His two hairy legs formed a wide-mouth, inverted U where they vised the pony's back. They joined at a narrow waist, which rose to support a barrel chest, then, with no visible neck to break the line, a hairless head the size of a large melon. His dark eyes, sunk deeply into his tiny head, regarded Ruth with an unblinking intensity that seemed devoid of any rationality, as a frog might watch a fly.

Ruth had no idea of how to react to the gaze, so she tried not to react at all. He stayed about three yards away from her and made no attempt to speak to her, if indeed he could speak, but the odor of the man-horse amalgam invaded her privacy and the unblinking stare attacked her nerves.

"That man is watching me," she whispered to Peter at the back of the wagon.

"Which man?"

"The short ugly man with no hat—and no hair. He keeps staring at me."

"Ignore him," Peter advised. "But keep an eye on him to see that he doesn't try anything. I'll watch him too."

"There's only a small amount of stuff left to pick up," said Mordecai, who had come up while they were talking. "Why don't you wait here, Ruth, and Peter and I will go pick it up. While we're doing this, he can explain to me how you can watch someone and ignore him at the same time."

Mordecai and Peter went out to gather in the few remaining

trade goods while Ruth stayed at the tail of the wagon, sorting and packing what was there. When all the goods were in, the bison boys walked their ponies forward and dismounted to collect their side of the bargain. Each of them took a share and strapped it to his back or his pony's back. One man carried the garlic clove, placing it carefully in a leather bag. Then they all went into a huddle again. After a couple of huddled minutes one of them broke out and galloped hell-for-blanket-pad toward the rest of the tribe. A minute later another one came out of the huddle and rode slowly over to the wagon.

He stopped about three yards away and held out his hand. "Friendship gift," he said. In the outstretched hand was a carved wooden jar filled with a yellow hard substance with a waxy sheen and an offensive odor. "Axle grease. Good for hair."

"Thank you," Mordecai said. He solemnly reached behind the collar of his jacket and pulled out a safety pin. "Friendship gift from us," he said, holding it out. The rider, just as solemnly, took it.

The rider who had split for the tribe was now heading back with a companion, and each of them had two ponies in tow. They pulled up with the rest of the group and one of them dismounted. He led the four ponies halfway to the wagon, where he stopped and looked expectant.

The rider next to the wagon, who had exchanged gifts with Mordecai, gestured toward the four ponies. "Horses," he said.

"Yes," Mordecai agreed. "Horses."

"We offer horses," the man said. "Four horses. Good price."

"Indeed it is," Mordecai said suspiciously. "For what?"

"Her," the man said.

"For her. Your daughter. Our boss wants your daughter. Offers four horses."

"Your boss?"

"John D. the Seventh." He pointed to the short, hairless man, who smiled a two-tooth smile and nodded vigorously. The rest of the bison boys, gathered around their boss, also nodded. One of them waved.

"Oh, no," Ruth said.

Peter started to stand, but Mordecai pushed him back. "There is a misunderstanding," he said. "This woman is not my daughter, she is my wife. Otherwise, of course, I would be honored at your offer."

"John D. wants her," the man said, explaining the facts of life to a stubborn child. "Six horses. You be good, no one gets hurt. Six horses fair. Buy new wife." He raised a hand and two riders started toward the wagon in a slow, deliberate walk.

"You misunderstand," Mordecai repeated. He dropped both hands casually under the seat and pulled at two concealed leather thongs. The shotgun dropped into his hands, and he pulled it out with his right and swung it across his lap so that it pointed in the general direction of the assembled bison boys. "This woman is mine. I do not sell what is mine. Nobody takes my woman away from me. Tell John D. to sleep with one of his horses tonight. Now you understand?"

"He would kill me," the man said, but both of his eyes were focused on the blue steel twin barrels of the shotgun. "We have one of those, but it hasn't fired in living memory. Will that one shoot?"

"Yes."

"Shoot it at something."

"No."

"Then it isn't loaded," the man decided with evident relief. "We will take the girl."

"You'll never know," Mordecai said, raising the gun so that it pointed squarely at the man's chest, "but your comrades will. Do you want them to find out? I'm not going to waste one of my two shells on a test."

"You kill me, the rest will rush you. You kill maybe one more. Then we take the girl. Kill you. Kill him."

"You'll never know about it," Mordecai said, keeping the gun pointed steadily at the man's chest. "And I'll get John D. with the second shot. Then I reload."

"Pah!" the man said, making a pushing gesture with his right hand. "Gun isn't loaded."

"Find out," Mordecai suggested.

The hairless man urged his pony a few steps forward and peered nearsightedly at the scene. "What happening?" he yelled. "You bring girl!"

"I talk to him," the man said, and backed away from the wagon.

The group went into a huddle again, and then spread out facing the wagon and took their unslung bows off their backs.

Mordecai stood up in the wagon seat and faced the bison boys. "Gentlemen," he shouted in a deep, clear voice. "I will, of course, kill the first man who slings his bow. But I do not wish to hurt anyone else, and this shotgun has a wide spray. So if the man next to you begins to sling his bow, move away from him or you may also be killed. I would regret that."

They all froze, and each man looked at his neighbor suspiciously. Then they went back into their huddle. At a whispered command the man holding the trade ponies went back to his own pony and mounted up.

The one who had spoken to them before came out of the huddle and faced them, keeping his distance. "She your wife?"

"Yes."

"Then she not virgin?"

"No."

"John D. not want girl who not virgin." He spat on the ground. "We go now. Our business is done."

"A pleasure doing business with you," Mordecai said. "It's good to see that the old American spirit of free enterprise isn't dead."

The group, slowly and with dignity, rode away. Their spokesman turned around after a few yards and stared at the wagon for a long moment. "It shoots?" he yelled.

Mordecai nodded. "It shoots."

He turned around and rode a few more yards. Then he stopped and turned back again. For about two minutes he said nothing. Then he yelled, "Watch out for Indians!" and turned around and rode off.

Ruth had been sitting, calmly and disinterestedly, between Mordecai and Peter. She maintained this pose until the group was well away from them, then she slumped and put her arm around Peter's waist. "Hold me," she said. "Just hold me!"

Peter pulled his arms out from under hers and pulled her to him. "It's over," he said. "Listen, Mordecai, I take back all my doubts about the shotgun—you were right. But you really had a lot of nerve to stand up to them with an empty gun. If they had called your bluff—"

"That kind of nerve I don't have whenever I don't have to,"

Mordecai said, cracking open the chamber of the gun and extracting two shells. "It's loaded."

"Where did you get the shells?" Ruth demanded. "Don't tell me that ammunition is seventy years old. You would have blown us all up if you'd fired it."

"It's hand-loaded," he said, hefting one. "Black powder. Would have made a hell of a lot of smoke and a hole the size of a dinner plate. Of course that's at four feet; at the distance that crew was I doubt if I could hit anything. They could have just stood back there and picked us off with arrows, if they'd a mind to."

"Why didn't they?" Peter asked.

"Moral superiority," Mordecai told him.

~~~~~~~~~~

16

They stopped for a week at the enclave in Denver. It still called itself the University of Denver and, wonder of wonders, maintained an active biology department. "You understand, it's not that they're really interested in it," Professor Happerman told Mordecai, "it's more that every well-rounded young scientist should be able to look at a chick-pea and think of Mendel. Or were they green peas?"

Professor Happerman was the head of the two-man biology department, and he had the look of a man who was always happy *despite* his environment. Mordecai looked at him in astonishment. "You mean you're still turning out scientists?"

"Well," Happerman looked uncomfortable, "not exactly. We train tinkers. It's part of our grand scheme."

"Not another grand scheme," Mordecai said. "Next you'll be calling yourselves the Proclave or the Autoclave." He frowned. "Tinkers?"

"Tinkers," Happerman assured him. "We send them forth in the world and they set up shop in small towns—or, for that matter, large towns—and fix things. If you're ever in trouble in a town with a tinker, let him know you're from an enclave, and he'll help you; if he's one of ours. And most are. Only don't give him away."

"I suppose you've got a secret handshake," Mordecai said, sounding delighted. "I'm particularly fond of secret handshakes."

"Well," Happerman said, "there's a password."

"Of course there is," Mordecai said. "What is it? 'Eureka'? 'Einstein'? 'Manhattan'? 'Binomial Theorem'?"

"You know, a lot of good people have put many years into setting this up," Happerman said. "We're trying to help keep the world from falling apart. It's not funny to us."

Mordecai put his arm around Happerman's shoulder. "As an old man, with the wisdom of much experience in what's left of this world," he said, "let me give you some very friendly advice: Don't ever lose your sense of humor. Believe me, the idea of a secret society of men dedicated to saving the world is funny. It's been funny for hundreds of years, and it's funny now; even though, for the first time, it might be true. And unless you people laugh at yourselves now and then, and keep laughing at yourselves, you're going to take yourselves seriously. Your little tinkers will become priests or something similar, with their superior knowledge. It's a small step from saving the world to ruling it. Particularly in the dreams of such savers who don't laugh. Now, what is that password?"

Happerman looked thoughtful. "I never—" he said. "You might— There are some indications. . . . Watson."

"Watson?"

"The password."

"Ah. As in 'Dr. Watson'? No, of course not! As in 'Watson, come here; I need you!'"

"I believe so. I'll begin making preparations to produce the serum right away, so we'll be ready when it arrives. If it arrives. Our legion of tinkers might prove very useful in distributing the vaccine to the people in the towns."

"It's a point," Mordecai said. "I was worried about that. They certainly wouldn't take it if it came from an enclave."

"Here they would," Happerman said. "The citizens of Denver are on very good terms with the university. But I know how rare that is."

Energy was no problem in Denver, as the electrical generators and hot-water boilers ran on locally mined coal. Peter and Ruth spent much of the week taking hot baths. The three of them went out to visit Lowry Air Force Base and look at the planes. "We think most of them are in flying condition," their guide, a seventeen-year-old undergraduate, told them. "Of course that's just a myth, since nobody here has any idea of how to fly one."

"That must really have been something," Peter said, staring at a giant cargo plane. "Who'd ever think that thing could fly?"

"It can't," Mordecai said sadly, "not anymore."

They walked silently down the row of parked and brooding airplanes. Ruth took Peter's hand in her left and Mordecai's in her right and they stood and stared out at the flat concrete surface of the runway. Grass was growing out of the cracks. Across the field a rusted radar antenna pointed south-south-east, as it had for the past seventy years.

"Let's go," Peter said. And they left.

Two days later they were on the road again. They made very good time for the next 150 miles, the first half downhill. The left rear tire gave out at the outskirts of Ogallala, in the Free State of Nebraska. It wasn't torn or punctured, it merely refused to hold air anymore. There was no way to patch it. The spare tire was inflated with the hand pump and installed, but Mordecai decided it was time to prepare for the end of the age of rubber.

The blacksmith in Ogallala was an earnest young man, but he confessed himself unequal to the task of fitting iron-shod wooden wheels onto the automobile hubs. Cutting plow blades out of ancient leaf springs was his closest approach to automotive mechanics.

Ogallala was a walled city—the first such they had seen. The road went right into the heart of town through gates that looked like they hadn't been closed in some years, but still the town was walled: a mottled masonry wall of stone, brick, and concrete block, twelve or more feet high, rectangled the town; wide enough to walk on, towered at the corners and the middles of the long sides. The gates at each end were also protected with towers. One of the corners angled into the Platte River, so that the tower in that corner was some ten yards out into the water.

"That wall is our history," the blacksmith told them. His smithy was built out from it, and it served as the back wall of his forge.

"How's that?" Mordecai asked. "It must be fairly recent; certainly since the Death."

"That's so," the smith agreed, "but it contains our past. It was built of all the unoccupied buildings in Old Ogallala. That's where the stone was, so that's where they quarried it."

They had to go on to North Platte to get their wagon rewheeled, but that would have to wait until tomorrow. Since they would have to spend the night in Ogallala anyway, they decided to put

on a show for the townspeople, and perhaps open them up to the
idea that travelers ain't all baddies who come to steal the town's
women and chickens.

They opened up the wagon for the show, and sent word out by
the small but intent band of preteen boys that had been following them around since they entered town. "Magic show," Mordecai told them. "Tell your folks. Nothing to buy. Just for fun. No,
scratch that. Tell your folks I said it's a lesson in moral humility
and goodness."

The stage occupied one long side of the wagon, and was fifteen
feet long and slightly over six feet deep. It had a canvas cover, canvas sides, and canvas skirting around the edge of the platform,
which was raised three feet off the ground. A half-size door had
been cut in the side of the wagon to connect with the stage when
it was up, but it blended in so well with the side that it effectively
disappeared when not in use.

This was a very small stage area to work on, and constant attention to detail was needed to keep it uncrowded with three people on it.

About 120 adults and easily twice as many children showed up
at the appointed time. The children gathered around the stage
and made the sort of loud and anticipatory noises that you would
expect from children. The adults clumped in a mass behind the
children and made no noises at all. They merely stared at the
empty stage, and their jaws worked rhythmically.

It was almost dusk and the wagon was faced into the setting
sun to minimize the shadows on the stage. The first evening
breezes were just beginning to stir at the skirts and trousers of the
crowd; slight breezes and low to the ground, and still warm from
the sun-baked earth, but pleasant and welcome nonetheless. The
crowd was not actively hostile, but it was clear that they were not
prepared to be pleased.

Peter and Ruth came out, went to opposite sides of the stage,
and sat cross-legged, facing the audience. They were dressed in
simple brown robes belted with rope, as novitiates in some unas-
suming coed monastic order might be.

Mordecai came out to center stage. His robe was black, with
threads of gold at the hems and a golden rope to belt it, and his
beard was trimmed and combed. His face was hooded by the cowl

of his robe and cast in shadow. He bowed low. "I welcome you to this performance of the Ancient Art," he told the audience, "as you have welcomed us to this town. I shall attempt to amaze and instruct you this evening as I show you some of the ancient wonders. These wonders were first described in the Bible, as practiced by the prophets of ancient Egypt and the Israel of David and Solomon, and by Moses himself as he led the Children of Israel out of bondage."

Mordecai stood up and stared evenly out at his audience. "First I should tell you, and you should remember well what I say, that there is nothing miraculous and nothing holy about my ability to perform these feats. Any man with a clear heart, who is without sin, who felt the calling and studied the Great Books and the Ancient Mysteries for twenty or thirty years, could become an adept, and another twenty years or so would suffice to make him a master. Beware of any man who attempts to tell you otherwise, to make of these God-given miracles more than they are. Any man who claims these powers and uses them for his own gain is a charlatan and should not be believed."

The audience stared, and even the children were silent. He had their attention, and now he had about two minutes to convince them before he lost it.

"How many of you read the Bible? Come on, let's see your hands. Don't be afraid to put your hand up if you read the Great Book—or have it read to you—you should be more ashamed to keep it down. That's right, that's better. Most of you, I see—all of you—including these little tykes here, who I'm sure are too young to read anything, even the Book. But you have it read to you, is that right? Your poppa reads it to you in the evening, after his hard day's work? Well, if he doesn't, perhaps he shall, perhaps he was just waiting until you were old enough to understand and appreciate that great work of man and God." Mordecai nodded and raised his hands as in a benediction.

"Cast your minds back to that wonderful time so long ago, in the land of Egypt, when Pharaoh ruled and the Children of Israel were in bondage. Pharaoh had magicians in his court, and they did tricks to keep him happy and to make him think they had great power. Like these . . ." And Mordecai took three small red balls from beneath his robe and began to juggle them high in the air.

The long rays of the sun glinted off the balls as they rose and fell in a weaving pattern. Peter and Ruth began to clap in time with the drop of the balls. In a few moments the children joined in the clapping.

A fourth ball joined the three, and then a fifth and sixth: a circle of whirling red spheres. Then the balls disappeared one at a time; back down to three, then two, then one lone ball, which vanished in Mordecai's hand.

"An ancient skill," Mordecai said, "which teaches dexterity, patience, and attention to detail; but certainly not magic." He took a large silver cup from a stand at the rear of the stage, and suddenly one of the red balls reappeared between the forefinger and index finger of his right hand. Then a second ball between the next two fingers, and a third ball, and a fourth, appearing in place as he waved his hand high in the air. "This," Mordecai told them, "on the other hand, is magic."

He made the balls disappear the way they had come, until there was only one left. This one he placed under the inverted silver cup on the stand. He snapped his fingers and suddenly there was a wand in his hand. Then he waved the wand over the cup and lifted it up. The ball had disappeared. The audience was impressed.

"Such are the tricks of the Egyptians," Mordecai said, tossing the ball to Peter and the cup to Ruth. "But they are as naught when compared to the skill of Moses, the wisdom of Solomon. Let me demonstrate." He nodded to his assistants, and they rose and brought forth two wooden saw-horses that had been concealed by the canvas sides of the stage. They were placed carefully parallel, about four feet apart, at the center of the stage.

Ruth turned to face Mordecai and Peter stood behind her. Mordecai removed a pendant with a bright red jewel from around his neck and slowly swung it back and forth before Ruth's eyes, murmuring softly to her as he did. Ruth closed her eyes and went rigid, her body stiff, and fell back into Peter's arms. Mordecai put the pendant back around his neck, stooped, and lifted Ruth by the feet.

Mordecai and Peter placed Ruth's rigid body on the two saw-horses, so that one supported her neck and the other her feet.

Mordecai turned to face the audience. "The magic of hypnosis," he told them. He went down to the very front of the stage and looked down at the sea of small faces that stared back at him. "What's your name, little man?" he asked one of the smaller faces.

"Mel."

"Hello, Mel. How old are you?"

"Five years old."

"Would you like to help me, Mel?"

"*Would* I!" Mel's eyes shone. "You just bet!"

Two adults in the back, evidently Mel's parents, made inarticulate, worried noises.

Mordecai lifted the little boy onto the stage. "My new assistant, Mel." He led the boy over to Ruth's horizontal body and, taking him by the elbows, stood him on top of her somewhere around the waist. "Stand tall!" he whispered. Mel stood tall.

There was the beginning of a murmur from the adult third of the crowd. There was a sort of hunching forward that brought them all a few feet closer to the stage.

Peter reached down and slowly removed the saw-horse that supported Ruth's feet. There was a gasp from the crowd as she *didn't* fall. The adults moved forward again, encroaching on the children's territory, staring in disbelief at the gravity-defying girl with the five-year-old standing on her stomach.

Mordecai stood behind Ruth and Peter brought him a large, silver hoop, which he held over her body. Peter went around to the one remaining saw-horse and, ever so gently, removed that one also.

Ruth now floated in mid-air, supporting a five-year-old boy. Mordecai passed the silver hoop over her head and down to her feet, telling Mel to duck under it when it reached him. Then he passed it back the other way and dropped it in the crook of his left arm.

The townspeople of Ogallala stared silently at the tableau before them, but they did not react. They had no idea of how to react; this was entirely outside of their experience. Before they could decide Peter returned the head saw-horse to its former position and lifted Mel down from his stomach perch. Then he returned the foot saw-horse and helped Mel off stage.

Mordecai lowered Ruth's feet to the floor and stood her up. Then he ran his hand over her eyes, which fluttered open; and she was awake, and once more supple, and not even a small boy could have safely stood on her stomach.

The troupe didn't take a bow; after all, this was a demonstration, not a performance. But at this point the demonstration was a decided success. If Mordecai hadn't made so many pointed references to the Bible at the beginning of the act, they would have decided by now that he was a witch. A few of them obviously thought so anyway; but a mob thinks with one mind, and the mob was awed and undecided.

Mordecai did a couple of simple effects more, but nothing to top the levitation or encourage the witch-hunters, and then it was too dark for further entertainment. The Ogallala farmfolk went off in sixes and sevens, discussing miracles and witchcraft. Mordecai and crew just dropped the front tent flap and crawled into their bedrolls, leaving the cleaning up for morning.

"Why didn't we try to sell them something?" Peter asked into the dark from his bedroll.

"What for?" Mordecai asked.

"Practice."

"Ah, Peter, Peter, you are developing a mercantile mind. Go to sleep! Or something." Mordecai rolled over and nothing further was heard until morning.

The next morning, while they were busy turning the stage back into a wagon wall, a delegation from the town, including a gaunt old man in ministerial black, approached somberly. The street was clear of all but the approaching four.

"Here it comes," Mordecai said in an undertone. "It only remains to see what it is. They've made up their minds about us."

"Well, the worst they can do is kick us out of town," Peter said, "and we're leaving anyway."

"You have an inexperienced and unfertile imagination," Mordecai told him, "a weak and flabby organ that needs more exercise."

Ruth giggled but made no comment.

The delegation paused at a respectful distance from the wagon. "Good morning," the minister said, making it sound like a benediction. "You are Mordecai?"

"I am," Mordecai admitted. "These are my assistants, Peter and Ruth. How may we help you?"

"I have heard reports of your—ah—demonstration last evening."
Mordecai nodded. "I hope they were favorable."

"Conflicting. As with all of life, no two opinions are the same."
The minister came up to the wagon. "I am Reverend Ditweiler.
Is this the stage?"

"It was. The canvas has all been stowed, but this is the platform.
The legs come off, and it slides into grooves in the floor of the
wagon."

"Ingenious," Reverend Ditweiler said. "And is this the young
lady who floated in mid-air above the whole audience for half an
hour last evening?"

Ruth gave a deep stage bow.

"The reports of Ruth's levitation have, I fear, been greatly exaggerated," Mordecai said. "But it was sufficient unto the occasion."

"Yes," Ditweiler said. "Illustrative, they tell me, of the book of
Exodus, and parts of Deuteronomy."

"Greatly exaggerated," Mordecai said.

Reverend Ditweiler sighed. "So I feared," he said. "You are preparing to leave Ogallala?"

"We should be gone within the hour," Mordecai told him.

"Good," the reverend said, nodding his head sharply. "If you
were to stay, I'd be forced to make the difficult choice of either
having you three burned at the stake or inviting you to speak in
my pulpit next Sunday morning. I confess I find both choices
equally unsatisfactory. I do not believe that the Lord works
through occasional miracles, and I doubt whether the Devil levi-
tates pretty girls in small towns in Nebraska Free State in his copi-
ous spare time. Your methods and your motives are equally
a mystery to me, and I think it would be best if you left town."
He shook hands firmly with Mordecai, Peter, and Ruth, in turn,
and then turned and walked back to his three companions and
accompanied them back down the street.

Mordecai and crew finished stowing the stage and then climbed
aboard the wagon and started off toward the great open gate in
the town wall. Even though it was well past dawn there was no
one on the street to watch them go. When they reached the gate
they found the first sign of activity: three men were oiling the
great hinges and the massive bolt, and cleaning out the track the
gate rode in.

"I think," Peter said when they were clear of the gate, "that they were trying to make sure we can't come back."

"I don't think they've used that gate in the past twenty years," Mordecai said. "They must have something in mind, and I'd very much like to know what."

"I imagine," Ruth said, staring at the wall of Ogallala as it shrank behind them, "that we'll find out."

~~~~~~~~~~

17

They traveled through the long summer day until dusk without seeing another human. They saw deer, and rabbits, and a beaver, and a long-tailed weasel, and a dust cloud in the distance that might have been caused by a group of men on horseback, or a family of moose, or a pride of lions for that matter. They camped that night by the side of the road, on the flat Nebraska plain, surrounded by the feral long grasses that immediately replaced fifty generations of hybrid corn in the absence of man.

They had no more than started the next morning when the walls of a town appeared in the distance ahead of them. A little over an hour later they had reached the walls, after traveling through about half a mile of a grid of checkerboard streets, with no buildings standing but an occasional foundation still peering up out of the dirt. The gate was a low, arched hole in the wall, wide enough for a wagon to pick which side to scrape, surmounted by a portcullis inset into the brick arch. A neatly painted sign, black letters on whitewashed wood, in the style of 1890s railroad stations, said:

NORTH PLATTE

A small group of men in fringed leather jackets and wide-brimmed, flat-top leather hats lounged about outside the gate. A small group of horses carrying identical McClellan saddles were hitched to a rail along the wall to the right of the gate.

"They're all dressed the same," Peter said, nodding toward the men.

"That's why it's called a uniform," Mordecai said.

"I always thought uniforms were those fancy things with brass buttons—like the costume I found."

"There's uniforms, and then there's uniforms," Mordecai said with less than his usual clarity. "Those gentlemen are all dressed the same because they're all members of the same military organization: army, police, or whatever they call it around here."

"What would these people need an army for?" Peter asked. "There aren't enough people in the world for anyone to have any reason to fight anyone else. I mean, if you want land, just start walking in some random direction until you reach some that isn't occupied."

"Oh?" Mordecai asked. "As simple as that, is it?" He put his hand on Peter's shoulder. "Tell me, why is the enclave of yours up on that hill? The townspeople hate you and cause you nothing but trouble. Why don't you just move twenty or thirty miles away?"

"But that's our home," Peter said. "We've always been there!"

"Historically inaccurate," Mordecai said, "but I understand your sentiment. Fight to keep it, would you?"

Peter thought about it. "Probably. But that's not fair. I mean, we're living there already. Why would anyone want to move in on us—or think that they had the right?"

"Ah, that's another question. Desires or rights are beyond the scope of the present discussion; the first is a psychological question, and the next is a philosophical problem. I was just trying to establish whether there was something *you* would fight for. Something territorial; I didn't want to get into that defending-your-wife-against-rape type of crap."

"You shouldn't defend your wife against rape?"

"Of course you should—and you should castrate the bastard who tries it—for the good of the race; but that's not a sound philosophical defense of war."

They pulled the wagon up to the gate, where a checkpoint had been established, and waited their turn to pass through into North Platte. There was a donkey cart ahead of them and a dreyer's wagon ahead of that. Each was being inspected by a pair of men, but it wasn't clear just what they were looking for.

One of the men in fringed leather, with some sort of stylized brass device pinned to his hat, came over to their wagon and consulted a piece of cardboard with a list neatly printed on it that he was holding in his left hand. "Number of people onboard," he demanded, "their names and acknowledged nationalities; point of origin of the wagon; intended destination; cargo, if any; reason for entering North Platte; location of residence or hostelry in North Platte; and the name of a citizen of North Platte, or of the Free State of Nebraska, who will give you a reference."

Mordecai leaned over and smiled down at him. "Good morning, Captain. Could we take those items one at a time, please?"

The man looked up at Mordecai with a bored expression in his angular face. "Names?"

"I am Mordecai Lehrer, and these are my children, Peter and Ruth."

"That's all?"

"Those are the only names we've got."

The look on the man's face turned to a scowl. "Are there any other persons aboard this wagon?"

"No, Captain, we are it, I'm afraid."

"Corporal. What was your point of origin?"

"California."

Now the soldier looked interested. "Over the mountains, eh? Very few make the trip anymore. Duchy or Los Angeles?"

"Duchy. Up around San Francisco Bay."

The soldier nodded. "Thought so. You can tell the ones from L.A. They all got this strange, fanatical look in their eye, and they smell like water is mighty scarce down there. Where are you headed?"

"All the way through to the New England Union. New York, as a matter of fact. Have business there. Corporal in what, if I may ask?"

"Citizens' Militia of the Free State of Nebraska," the corporal said, reaching up to finger the brass device on his hat. "This is our signal."

"What is it?" Ruth asked.

"An ear of corn. Nebraska is the corn-husker's state. Not much grown anymore, but it's our signal." He looked up with interest at Ruth, who had been hidden behind Mordecai until she leaned forward. "And this," he told her, pointing to a thin, red double-chevron painted on his upper sleeve, "is my insignia. It means I'm a corporal." He was obviously very pleased about being a corporal.

"I thought stripes like that were sewed on," Mordecai said. "Isn't that the tradition?"

"I don't know anything about that," the corporal said, "but you don't sew any more than you have to through a leather jacket, you don't. Not if you want it to stay waterproof."

"A point," Mordecai admitted. "It's a pleasure to know you, Corporal." He offered his hand.

The corporal shook it, but his eye was on Ruth. "Stacy," he said. "Corporal Henry Stacy. Going to stay here in North Platte long, are you?"

"Just passing through," Peter growled.

"As a matter of fact," Mordecai said, "we will be here a few days. We need a wheelwright, or at least a blacksmith, and the smithy here has been recommended by the young smith back in Ogallala."

"A few days," Corporal Stacy said. "You might be here longer than that, you know."

"What do you mean, Corporal?" Mordecai asked. "Isn't a man free to come and go as he pleases in the Free State of Nebraska?"

"Of course," Stacy said. "And that's just the point: we're trying to see that you keep that privilege. That's what we're fighting for: the right of every man to think as he pleases, travel as he pleases, vote as he pleases, worship as he pleases—as long as he keeps it within reasonable bounds. This is assured by the Constitution of the Free State of Nebraska, which document I am sworn to uphold. After all, our state motto is, 'Equality Before the Law,' isn't it?"

"Fighting who?" Mordecai demanded.

"The Simples. They're trying to come up through Kansas—cut the state in half with a flying column like Sherman did to the Confederacy. Then they'll invade in force through Iowa; probably up around Sioux City. Latest word is the column has reached the Platte River south of Kearney. Now they'll probably take 183 north or 80 east, but if they head west on 80 or 30, you're going to be here for a while."

"Who's that you're fighting?" Mordecai asked. "Who or what are the Simples? And, if you'll excuse my being blunt, why should your fight with them concern us? We're not Nebraskans, and have little interest in who controls what land in what state. I don't mean to offend you—"

"Boy, you really are from California, aren't you?" the corporal commented. "Look, let me explain, if I can. You know who the Simples are?"

"No."

"Well . . . the gentleman in charge of the United States of America right now—a country which is made up of the old states of Kansas, Missouri, Iowa, Illinois, and, I think, parts of Indiana and Oklahoma—is a dude who calls himself Brother Simon. He has a divine calling to unite the scattered remnants of the old US of A into one great country; under his leadership, of course. His followers are called the Simples. They call themselves that, you understand. I would say it's an accurate description, but I guess I'm prejudiced. So they're on this holy crusade to take over the rest of the continent, starting with Nebraska."

"It sounds dreadful," Mordecai agreed, "but I still don't see what it has to do with us. We're not fighters, after all."

"Well," Corporal Stacy said, pushing his hat back on his head, "you impress me as the sort of man who could survive anywhere; but would you really like to bring your kids up as Simples?"

"What is the, ah, Simplist doctrine?" Peter asked.

"Simply stated," Corporal Stacy said, grinning, "it is: 'Brother Simon knows best.' Blind faith and obedience, and perpetual war on your neighbors, is what Brother Simon knows. Based on the theory that everything from the 'Golden Age' is the work of Satan and must be destroyed. And they've been going around methodically doing just that. Nasty people. Not, you understand, that I have any use for the so-called science of the Golden Age; but some of the gadgets are useful, if you can get them to work."

"But we have to get through to the East," Mordecai said. "What will they do to us if we try to pass through their territory?"

"Hard to predict," Corporal Stacy said. "Logic and consistency are not their strong points. They may let you through with no trouble at all. They may shoot you on sight. If I were a betting man, and it not forbidden in the service, I'd give three to two on the latter."

"Very cheerful," Mordecai said. "I will have to think on it."

"Yes. Well, while you're thinking let me fill out the rest of my paper. What's your cargo?"

"Odds and ends," Mordecai said. "Personal belongings and paraphernalia, and a few hundred bottles of snake-oil elixir, good for everything from halitosis to dermatitis. We sell it in our spare time, when we're not educating the public."

"Hum," Corporal Stacy said, writing with the stub of a thick pencil. "Nothing of value? No weapons?"

"An ancient shotgun of dubious value," Mordecai said.

"No modern weapons?" the corporal asked. "No crossbows, recurve bows, muzzle-loaders, or other projective weapons of recent manufacture?"

"Nary a one," Mordecai said.

"Any Nebraskan who'll vouch for you?"

"Nary a one," Mordecai said.

The corporal did a cursory search of the wagon, and then handed them a ticket of clearance. "This is good for two days," he said, "but can be extended for cause by the lieutenant of the guard. I suggest the Goldenrod Inn."

"Nicest hotel in town, is it?" Mordecai asked.

"Only hotel in town," the corporal said. He touched his hand to the brim of his hat. "Excuse me, ma'am," he said to Ruth. "I get off duty at fourteen hundred hours. Could I feel free to call on you and show you the sights of the town, such as they are? With your father's permission, of course."

Ruth nodded gravely. "I would be delighted, Corporal Stacy. Thank you for asking me."

Mordecai guided the horses slowly through the narrow entranceway, past the gate, and out onto West Twelfth Street, headed toward the center of town. The area inside the walls was spacious and uncrowded, and the streets were wide and comfortable for wagon traffic. They were tree-lined and peaceful-looking.

"They seem to have covered a lot of area with that wall," Mordecai said, looking back at the straight, stone line, three stories tall, that stretched out behind them. "It must have been a lot of work for someone. I wonder who."

Peter was glaring at Ruth. "What did you mean you'd be delighted to go out with that corporal?" he demanded.

Ruth looked at him and did not answer.

"Well," he repeated, "what did you mean?"

"Peter!" Ruth said. "What was all that talk about trusting each other, and knowing we loved each other even if we saw other people? We spent nights talking about that. It seems to me we spent months talking about that. And I didn't even want to see anyone else."

"And now you do?" Peter asked.

"What was I supposed to say to him?" Ruth asked. "And what do you mean: it's all right for me to go out with someone else as long as I don't want to? Is that what you mean? That doesn't make sense."

"But a goddamn corporal in the goddamn Nebraska militia; him you want to go out with? And you've seen him for maybe a minute? *That* doesn't make sense!" Peter crossed his arms and kept glaring as his voice rose.

Ruth shifted in the seat and turned to glare at him and her voice matched his. "What do you think—I lust after him? You think I want his body? What the hell do you think I'm going to do with him tonight? It's kind of a nice feeling when a man you've never seen before can't take his eyes off you, and then asks you out. As long as he's polite."

"I wouldn't know," Peter said. "Mordecai, what the hell did you have to tell him we were your kids for? That makes us brother and sister."

"It seemed the sensible and safe thing to do," Mordecai said. "Less explanation required. And it still does. And if you two don't keep your voices down I'm going to kick you both off the wagon and pretend I never saw you before."

"You're right," Ruth said, her voice dropping to normal level. "It's silly. It's a stupid thing to have a fight about."

Peter turned to stare at some distant object off to the right. "You mean you're not going to go out with him?"

"I mean no such thing. Of course I'm going out with him. I promised, didn't I?"

"Well," Peter said, "I don't think it's a good idea. Suppose something happens? Suppose he finds out you're from an enclave? Suppose he tries to rape you, or something?"

"Then I'll scream, and scream, and kick him in the crotch," Ruth said. "Don't be so solicitous about me; I can take care of myself."

Peter kept staring off into space and said nothing further. Ruth turned and stared off in the other direction. Mordecai, sitting between them, looked from one to the other. "Great," he said. "I'm traveling with a pair of bookends."

The hotel was an ancient four-story building on Jeffers Street that was in amazingly good condition for its age. It had working bathrooms, running water, and a wood-burning water boiler that brought hot water right to the tap in two of the bathrooms (and, the landlady told them, the kitchen, which was a great convenience). It was kept hot for three or four hours a day, usually in the evening. There was a constant bicker between those who preferred the hot water in the morning and those who wanted it in the evening, among the hotel's staff and guests; but at the moment the evening people were in the ascendency.

Their room, the last empty room the Goldenrod Inn had to offer, was a large one on the second floor, front, overlooking the large stable across the street. It was crammed full of beds, so close together that they had to go sideways between them, when they could fit between them at all. There were twelve beds in the room, and one bureau, one washstand, one ancient stuffed chair, and a standing lamp which had once been electric but now held a pint of oil and a wick. The walls were decorated with framed photographs of men standing by the sides of racecars and smiling, of racecars racing, and one of a group of men standing together and smirking at the camera with a large trophy of some sort standing in front of them. The writing across the bottom identified them as the winners of the Cody Memorial Bowling League Trophy for 1992. There were also three identical oil paintings of the Grand Canyon.

Peter tossed his bundle of belongings on the nearest bed and stared at the rest of them. "They've given us the orgy room," he decided finally.

"More likely the storeroom," Mordecai said, tossing his pack onto a bed in the corner. A small cloud of dust rose where the pack had landed, verifying his suspicions. "She said they were full up except for this room. Must be a storeroom, used for guests only in the unlikely happening that they're full up."

Ruth picked a bed near the window and settled down on it. "I had so looked forward to a room of my own, just for this once," she said. "And they had to be full for the first time in a hundred years. It's discouraging."

"I know," Mordecai said. "Privacy is a wonderful thing when you're deprived of it. Of course, if you have too much of it, it's called solitary confinement. Man is a funny animal."

"You just want to get away from me, is that it?" Peter demanded, glaring across at Ruth.

"That's the most asinine thing you've ever said to me," Ruth said, putting her hands on her hips and glaring back at him. "The most!"

"Excuse me, kiddies," Mordecai said, "but I think I'll go downstairs for a while and stretch my legs. Rest my ears a bit, too. You two keep it up for as long as you've a mind to, but please keep it down. And remember: you're supposed to be brother and sister, and we'll all get in a hell of a lot of trouble if anyone around here finds out any different." He stopped in the hall and turned back in before closing the door. "At your leisure, one of you might join me downstairs and help me take the wagon over to the wheelwright." He closed the door softly behind him.

The walk downstairs to the lobby answered the question of why the hotel was full for the first time in living memory: soldiers of all sizes, ages, ranks, and specialties passed him on the stairs and in the lobby, apparently coming in from maneuvers. Most of them had crossbows slung on their backs, but there were a few longbows and recurve bows, and one squad of men had lever-action rifles. Mordecai was curious about the ammunition supply for the rifles, but didn't feel like being hanged for spying. He had no idea of how sensitive the local military was to questions, so he didn't ask.

He spent about ten minutes in the lobby watching the soldiers straggle in, then he noticed a pair of officers who seemed to be watching him. At least he assumed they were officers; they had rolls of thick yellow rope around the brims of their hats and carefully cultivated airs of command. Rapidly assuming the best defense, he approached the two. "Afternoon," he said, touching the brim of his dilapidated felt hat. "You two gentlemen billeted here?"

"Afternoon, sir," the one on the left replied. "Name's Mollet, Captain Mollet. Pleasure, sir. This here's Captain Sterling." He offered his hand. "Not from around here, are you?" He did his best to make the question sound casual.

Aha! Mordecai thought, *Military Intelligence, as I live and*

breathe. And doing their subtle best, so I mustn't discourage them.
"I'm merely a fellow guest at the hotel," he told them. "Fresh from
California. Northern California: the Duchy of. Crossing the coun-
try selling medications and entertaining the populace."

"Come from the West then, have you?" Captain Sterling asked.
He was a short, balding man with a neatly clipped mustache
above a thin-lipped mouth, an angular nose, and small, close-set,
mean-looking eyes. He clipped his words and gestures, and turned
precise corners, and gave the impression that one day he would
go off and demolish the immediate area. "Must have been on
the road awhile then. Not many hotels out that way. Come
through Scottsbluff, did you? Stop there at all?"

"We missed Scottsbluff," Mordecai told him. "Came along 80.
Just came from Ogallala yesterday." He tried to look earnest and
sincere, and as though he didn't notice the air of interrogation
accompanying the friendly questions.

"Ogallala," Captain Mollet mused. He was taller and more
rounded off than Sterling. He had the bumbling, friendly look of
a brown bear, and was probably just as dangerous. His tones had
the broad *a* of the Midwest, which made him sound relaxed and
slow-witted; but the spark of intelligence was deep set into his
brown eyes. "There just yesterday, were you?"

"That's right."

"You the fellow that did the magic show?"

"That's right. Word sure gets around. They must have liked it."

"That sure was a nice thing for you to do," Mollet said. "I mean,
doing that magic show for those people and then not even trying
to sell them anything. That was sure a nice thing to do."

"We like to do nice things for people, Captain. It gives us pleasure to see other people happy." Mordecai thought he saw where
Mollet's line of thinking was taking him, and wanted to get there
first.

"Sure was nice," Captain Mollet repeated. "Can't make much
of a living, being nice to people."

"In the entertainment business, that's called 'good will,' Captain. The people weren't very receptive to us when we came to
town, so we gave them a free show. Now they'll remember and
be nice to us when we come back through. It didn't cost us any-

thing, not even time—we were going to spend the night there anyhow."

Mollet nodded his head. "Makes sense," he admitted. "Still, it sure was nice of you. Always get suspicious when someone does something nice for no apparent motive. Figure somewhere down there he's got a motive hidden, and I want to know what it is. Caught me a spy that way once: he was just being too damn nice."

"Coming through Wyoming," Captain Sterling asked, "you happen to see anything of a herd of buffalo they got up there?"

"The bison? Almost ran headlong into them. Took about half a day for them to pass the wagon, and we had to keep moving to stay out of their way."

"That's what I heard," Sterling said, looking wistful. "Got to get up there someday. Got to shoot me a buffalo."

"No great trick if you can find them," Mordecai said. "There's a group of men, a kind of nomadic tribe, living by following the herd. Not very civilized, but they seem to be surviving. They'll trade for hides, meat, and the like."

"Indians?" Captain Mollet asked.

"Nope. As a matter of fact, they warned me about the Indians. I think I would have preferred the Indians."

"Probably remnants of the crazies," Sterling said. "Might be worthwhile to go up there sometime and shoot a couple of them."

"The crazies?" Mordecai asked.

"Tell me you don't know about the crazies?" Mollet asked.

"I'm telling you."

"That's why the walls were put up around these towns: the crazies and the randoms."

"I thought it was this war you're having with the US of A."

"Hell, Simple Simon wasn't anywhere around fifty years ago when the wall went up. Well, he might have been around, but he was still clinging on to his mama's teat. No, it was to protect them from the crazies mostly. Bands of them would come through about three or four times a year and"—he waved his hand vaguely—"do things."

"What things?" Mordecai asked.

"It was hard to predict. That's why we called them 'crazies.' Bunch of them came through once and held everyone in town at gunpoint while they broke all the television sets into flinders. Said the radiation from the television was what caused the Death. Then they rode off. Mind you, this was maybe twenty or thirty years after the last TV station went off the air, and about as long after the last generator broke down. Another bunch tried to drown everyone they found who wasn't baptized. Then there were the ones who ate human livers."

"Livers?" Mordecai asked.

"I remember them from when I was a kid. We thought it was the liver, it was hard to tell. We'd find these bodies on the road all hacked up, and there'd be a cookfire nearby. We went after that group and shot them all—my folks did, I mean. I remember that especially because it was the last of the real ammunition: brass cases and primers and smokeless powder and jacketed bullets. That was way after the wall went up, of course."

"That's incredible," Mordecai said.

"You mean you didn't have crazies in California?"

"Only in southern California, and not the type you're describing. People in the Central Valley moved over to the coast and set up little communities in the shadows of deserted cities like San Francisco and Oakland. And, of course, there are the enclaves."

"Talk about strange people!" Captain Sterling said.

"Oh? Ah, troublesome, are they?" Mordecai asked.

"No, not that way," Mollet said. "They just want to be left alone. Very retrograde types. Insist on hanging on to the old ways, for all the good it does them. Find them useful, though; they're the only ones with enough of the old skills to keep some of our gadgets working."

"What sort of gadgets?" Mordecai asked.

"Ah, hum—" Captain Sterling said.

"Well," Captain Mollet said, waving his hand vaguely about, "gadgets. This and that. Enclave at Fullerton produces most of the hybrid grown in the state."

"Hybrid?"

"Corn. Then there's the one at Lincoln. That's the, ah, the other one."

"Surely, Captain," Mordecai said, staring intently at Mollet, "you don't think I'm a US of A spy, do you?"

"Nope," Captain Mollet said. "The Simples aren't interested in the enclaves. When they capture one, they usually burn it to the ground." He met Mordecai's stare. "To the ground, Mr. Lehrer."

"You seem to be putting strong emphasis on this act of barbarism, Captain Mollet," Mordecai said, keeping his voice casual as his mind raced. Point: he had *not* mentioned his name to the captains. Point: they connected him with the enclaves. Point: they must have gotten his name from that corporal at the gate, fine; but why would they want him to know that they were interested in him? They wouldn't say anything like that by accident. There was but one way to find out. "Also, if I may say so, I seem to detect a strong interest in myself and my affairs; an interest that would hardly seem to be warranted by the circumstances of my arrival and my evident innocence of involvement in your current problems. May I ask why?"

"I'll have to sort that question out, sir," Mollet said. "If you'll give me a second to review—"

"Why are we interested in your affairs?" Captain Sterling said. "It's our job, you know, to be interested in everything that goes on within fifty miles of here."

"I don't think that was the man's question, Sterling," Mollet said. "If I have it sorted out properly, he wants to know why he has detected this strong interest; which is an entirely different matter." He looked respectfully at Mordecai. "We were just checking your reaction, sir. And a waste of time that was. You *are* from one of the enclaves, aren't you?"

Mordecai thought about it for a moment, then mentally shrugged and flipped a coin. "Sort of," he said.

"We thought so," Captain Sterling said, glaring menacingly at Mordecai. "We thought so!"

"First of all," Captain Mollet said, "you're carrying a load of books. There's a double floor on your wagon that's cram-full of books."

"Insulation," Mordecai said.

"No doubt. And cases of books everywhere there's room; cases made especially to fit into the odd corners and lie flat under the bunks. Books are a very heavy cargo; and you can't eat a book, or plant a book, or shoot a book, or wear a book, or trade a book to anyone I know. About the only thing a book's good for over most of this country is heat, and I imagine you wouldn't lug them this far just to get them burned."

"Clearly," Mordecai agreed.

"So you're taking them from one 'clave to another, the way we figure."

"That's right."

"And those little kits with the test tubes and stuff," Captain Sterling said, "what are they for—some of them scientific experiments?" He said the word "scientific" the way an earlier generation might have said "pornographic."

"I'm afraid my associate is imbued with the contemporary ethic," Mollet said, shaking his head sadly. "But then, of course, there's this. . . ." He lifted a rough leather case from where it rested by his feet, opened a flap, and pulled out one of the microfiche packets that had been concealed along the wall of the wagon. He opened the packet and removed a microfiche card. Holding it between thumb and forefinger, he extended it toward the window so that the sunlight came through, lighting it with a rosy glow.

"Be careful with those," Mordecai said. "They're far older than you are, and much more fragile."

"I recognize the beasts," Mollet said. "But what information do they contain? What valuable knowledge are you transporting?"

"I was about to compliment you on the efficient searching of my wagon," Mordecai said. "You mean you didn't find the viewer?"

"If so my men didn't know what it was," Mollet told him.

"So. Let's hope they didn't tear things apart too much," Mordecai said. "Come on, I'll find it and show you." He walked out to the wagon with the two captains and climbed aboard. Mordecai looked carefully around but could detect no sign of the comprehensive search the wagon must have just undergone. "Your men are good, Captain," he said.

"Better be," Mollet replied.

Mordecai found the hand viewer and opened it. "Look through this end," he told Mollet, "and slide the card in there."

"I don't see anything," Mollet commented.

"Hold it up to the light."

"Oh, right. I see. *Life on the Mississippi*, it says here. That the same man who wrote *Tom Sawyer?*"

"That's right."

"Read that when I was a kid. Father made me learn how to read. Had piles of old books. Some fell apart as you turned the pages. *Tom Sawyer* was one of my favorites. Also *Tarzan and the Jewels of Opar*. You mean these micro-things are all just more books?"

Captain Sterling kicked disgustedly at one of the cartons of books. "Packrats!" he snorted.

"Just so, Captain," Mordecai agreed. "We're attempting to save these books because we feel that they should be saved. No greater reason."

"Perhaps reading will come back someday," Captain Mollet said. "I enjoyed it as a boy. But then I was a lonely child. Keep your trinkets, Mr. Lehrer, and good luck to you; but expect no pity from the Simples if you run afoul of them."

"You mean we can leave when we're ready?"

Mollet shrugged. "That was never up to us, sir. We hold no man against his will without just cause. That protection is guaranteed in the Constitution of the Free State of Nebraska." He gave Mordecai a vague salute, then he and Sterling went back into the hotel.

A few minutes later Peter came out. He was not looking happy. He was looking angry and determined, but not happy. Ruth was still planning to go out with Corporal Stacy. Peter tried to get Mordecai to agree with him that she was wrong, but Mordecai retreated into philosophy, and so they spent the short ride to the smith's in absolute silence. Peter pulled the wagon up outside and they went in.

"Wheels? Sure," the smith said. "Let's get a look at your rig." He was a short, stocky man with upper arms and thighs grown massive with the work they'd been put to. He had an intelligent, slightly quizzical expression on his face.

When he reached the wagon parked outside his door he walked around it twice silently, and then a third time muttering to himself. "Not from around here, are you?" he asked finally, stopping in front of Mordecai.

"Not nearly," Mordecai said. "What's the trouble?"

"No trouble," the smith said. "I just never did see a rig like that. Not only the rubber tires, but the brakes inset into the wheel, and those air cylinders—shock absorbers are they?—and the springs, and the tolerances. . . . I didn't think things like this were possible anymore. *I* can't match it—I can't do the machining. It's all from before the Death, isn't it? Don't expect me to believe that anyone is doing this kind of work today!"

"There was a big military depot where we came from," Mordecai told him. "A lot of the stuff was packed in such a way that it was protected from the passage of time: no rusting, no aging. Unfortunately, the tires rot no matter how well they're packed."

"Well," the smith said, biting at his lower lip and staring at the wagon, "I can fit wheels onto those hubs for you. Take me about four days; I got some back contracts to clean out first. My assistant just married and moved to Broken Bow to open his own shop, and my only half-trained apprentice just ran off and joined the army. My only other boy is learning how to sweep the floor. I give him another couple of months, he'll have it down. So it's going to take me a bit longer than it would normally. Figure four days."

"That's fine," Mordecai said. "That's better than we hoped."

"How you planning to pay for this?" the smith asked.

"I was just getting to that," Mordecai said. "What's it going to cost, and what sort of specie do you favor?"

The smith rested his chin in his hands and began tapping the end of his nose with his forefinger. "Well," he said, "I figure over half a day each of the next four days—five days actually, I don't work on Sunday—building your wheels. That's the best part of a week. You're not planning to pay in grain, or chickens, or the kind, are you?"

"No, sir," Mordecai said. "Cash-type money. Silver."

"I could use some," the smith commented. "The people around here have damn little, and I have to pick up supplies from the dreyers, who want nothing else. Let's say twenty dollars, silver. Washington dollars, or a ten-cents-on-the-dollar boost for any local money."

"Fair enough," Mordecai said. "Twenty-two Duchy of California dollars it is. Do you want advance payment, or something on account?"

"No need," the smithy said. "You're not going anywhere until I'm done."

Corporal Stacy came to call for Ruth when he got off duty that evening, and they went for a walk along the bank of the North Platte. Peter sulked in the room. The next day Corporal Stacy came to call for Ruth and took her for a walk along the bank of the South Platte (the town rests in the fork of the two rivers), and Peter sulked in the room. The next day was Sunday, and Corporal Stacy was off duty. He invited Ruth, and her father and brother, to join him at the company mess for Sunday dinner.

"I won't go," Peter said.

"You're joking!" Ruth said. "I keep thinking you'll be over your jealous attack, but you never are."

"I keep thinking you won't go out with the corporal again," Peter said, "but you always do. I thought once was enough to make your point."

"I'm not trying to make a point," Ruth said, "except that I have the right to go out with anyone I please."

"Suppose I pick up some local girl," Peter said; "then how would you feel?"

"You have that right," Ruth told him. "That's the point, if there is one."

"You're only saying that because you know that Nebraska mothers don't let their daughters go out with vagrant wagoneers," Peter said, but he agreed grudgingly to go to the dinner.

They dressed in their best, cleanest, and least-patched clothes for the occasion, and Peter and Mordecai even carefully trimmed their beards with barber's scissors before they left the room.

Peter became very quiet as he stared in the mirror and manipulated the scissors. Then, as they left the room, he took Ruth's hand. "I figured out what it is," he told her.

"What?"

"I'm partly jealous of you going out with someone else instead of me," he told her. "But even more than that, I just realized, I'm jealous of you going out with someone else when I don't have anyone else to go out with. Does that make sense? I realized it when I started talking about Nebraska girls and their mothers."

Ruth kissed him—after looking around to make sure that nobody could see the sibling affection—and squeezed his hand. "I'm
glad you figured that out," she said. "I don't like making you feel
bad, but I couldn't see any way around it if I was going to stay
honest with myself and my beliefs. I'm glad you won't be jealous
anymore."

"I didn't say that," Peter said. "And I don't mean I'm going to
be completely happy about your going out with someone else, but
I guess I can live with it now. There's another thought that keeps
bothering me. Do you know how stupid it is of me to be suffering
these horrible pangs of jealousy—probably the strongest emotion
I've ever felt except for that night in jail—over your going out with
another man? I mean, the odds are good that none of us are going
to be alive ten years from now. The whole human race is probably
doomed, and this one male human animal is angry because his
female is rubbing noses with another male. It's sick!"

"You sound like Mordecai," Ruth said, "except that his imagery
would be better, and he's never so negative. You sound like Peter
Thrumager after two months' exposure to Mordecai, I guess.
Rubbing noses! And you'd better be quiet about that; we
shouldn't let anything about the—problem—be overheard here."

"Right," Peter whispered. "Quiet morbidity, that's the way."
And he silently escorted her downstairs to where Mordecai was
waiting for them in the lobby.

The dinner, served at four in the afternoon, when all good din-
ners should be served, was roast chicken and biscuits and roast
corn and butter and green salad, with pitchers of cold milk, and
hot apple pie for dessert. Afterward small ceremonial glasses of a
very hard cider were passed around, and there were after-dinner
toasts and welcomings and speeches and introductions and sober
appraisals and unsteady estimates and backslappings and one near
fistfight between two lieutenants which was broken up by a corporal who interposed himself between them and pointed out that
it was against military regulations for an officer to strike an en-
listed man.

All through the meal, and the dessert, Captains Mollet and
Sterling kept eyeing Mordecai and whispering between themselves. It was beginning to make Mordecai nervous, and he was
contemplating some form of direct action when Captain Mollet

removed the need by coming over. "May I join you?" he asked
ceremoniously.

Ruth and Peter had just left their seats by Mordecai to join
in an attempt to squaredance to the music of two bugles, a bag-
pipe, and a snare drum, and Mollet straddled the seats they had
vacated, facing Mordecai.

"Join me," Mordecai said, starting on his second piece of pie.
"I insist."

"We would like you to do us a favor," Captain Mollet said.

"Who is 'us'?" Mordecai asked. "I'm afraid to ask what the favor is."

Captain Mollet considered the question. "Us is the Militia of
the Free State of Nebraska, the people of the state, the common
good of humanity wherever it survives, and all those other loaded
phrases we're supposed to be fighting for."

"That's a heavy load to lay on one man, Captain. I don't know
if I can handle a favor as heavy as that."

"The favor itself is quite simple," Captain Mollet said. "We
would like you to deliver a letter for us."

"Where to?"

"An address in Lincoln."

"Lincoln," Mordecai said. "Is Lincoln under Simple control or
yours?"

"Still under free-state control, to the best of our knowledge,"
Captain Mollet said.

"Then what's the problem?"

"The Simples are between us and Lincoln," Mollet said.
"There's a good chance that by the time you get to Lincoln the
Simples will be there. They've driven a wedge up 281 through
Grand Island. Probably up as far as O'Neill now. The Seventh
Regiment is supposed to be between them and Lincoln, but their
orders are to fall back behind Lincoln and protect Omaha."

"I think I need a map to follow this," Mordecai said. "Why
aren't you protecting Lincoln, or is that classified information?"

"Of course it is," Captain Mollet said. "All of this is classified
information. If the Simples knew that they could take Lincoln
without a fight, they'd move in. The main body of the Seventh
is sitting between them and Lincoln to keep their thoughts directed north. But Lincoln isn't really worth defending, for stra-

tegic reasons. We have to make our stand at Omaha. But there's this, ah, gentleman in Lincoln whom we have to get certain data to."

"What is this letter?" Mordecai asked.

"Nothing much," Captain Mollet said. "Just a letter. Very innocuous if anyone happens to read it. I don't think you'd want to know more than that anyway."

"If it looks like trouble with the Simples, I'll just burn the letter or eat it, or something," Mordecai warned. "My needs are greater to me than yours."

"Of course they are," Captain Mollet agreed. "Of course you will."

Mordecai sighed. "Oh hell," he said, "give me the letter."

18.

~~~~~~~~~~~~

Odysseus entered Earth orbit like a pebble returning to the sling. With only the slightest nudge—a four-second burst from the ten-newton thruster—the ship slowly fell toward the spot where *Quetzalcoatl*, Feathered Serpent, would catch up and the docking maneuver, that strange, mechanical mating dance, would be performed for the first time in seventy-three years.

Socrates Proudfoot methodically completed the docking checklist, reading aloud each item, performing the required action, then checking the number off with a red felt-tip. The air inside *Odysseus* was becoming increasingly clammy and damp—the dehumidifier was malfunctioning in some undisclosed manner—and Socrates quietly thanked whatever random force had brought *Odysseus* and the giant space station together before the fog in his cabin had coalesced and it had begun to rain. The life processes in a closed environment essentially produce more water than they consume. The facilities aboard *Quetzalcoatl* would enable him to repair or replace the defective unit before he started the long trip home. Even though it would be a complex and frustrating task for one person alone, it would be possible; and thus it would be done.

Odysseus fell into the shadow of *Quetzalcoatl* and a programmed half-second burst from the secondary booster matched velocities to within the limits of his instruments. Then, after studying the relative positions of the two artifacts, Socrates fired a two-second puff from one of the trim tubes, and they closed.

It took Socrates one pass around *Quetzalcoatl* before he was able to spot the ship's dock mechanism. He had expected a featureless expanse of metal except for the dock and a couple of airlocks; instead, the surface of the great space station was mottled

and speckled with docks, locks, shades, small fabric-covered frameworks, large uncovered frameworks, parabolic mirrors, flat mirrors
in rows, in stacks, in grids, and one cubical array. One set of mirrors turned as the station turned, still faithfully tracking the sun
in idiot obedience to its hundred-year-old instructions.

Socrates guided *Odysseus* cautiously to the ship dock, playing
the controls with the fine touch of a man who grudges the waste
of an erg of energy. The two couplings met and pressed together
but they refused to mate. Three times Socrates completed the
docking maneuver, and three times the couplings didn't complete.

Socrates Proudfoot released the catch on the webbing that held
him into the pilot's seat, stretched his body out, arms and legs
wide, and allowed the momentum to send him floating into the
center of the small cabin. Then, using the psychomotor techniques
taught to every Martian child, he relaxed every muscle in his body
from the extremities inward, and focused all his attention into a
little white ball of consciousness somewhere inside his head. His
heartbeat slowed, his blood pressure dropped, and his breathing
slowed to six breaths a minute. In this attitude, which decreased
his demand on the life-support systems, to a minimum, he concentrated all of his attention on his problem. *Odysseus* languidly
pulled away from the docking mechanism and drifted, millimeter
by millimeter, away from *Quetzalcoatl*.

The problem was complex: If it were just Socrates entering the
space station, there'd be no problem, since he'd have to enter in
a lifesuit anyhow. All the air in the habitat had surely dissipated
by now, and would have to be replaced from the tanks. But Socrates needed the ability to bring complex and massive equipment
back aboard *Odysseus* to get it checked out, re-outfitted, and cali-
brated, and get the life-support systems recharged for the trip
back to Mars. Having *Odysseus* on the end of a tether wouldn't
do—she had to be immediately and conveniently accessible from
the station, and the only answer was some form of docking. All
this was dependent, of course, on Spaceport Chicago's being able
to keep their part of the bargain and come up with some way to
refuel the shuttle. But that was something Socrates had no control
over, so he didn't waste time thinking about it.

Socrates stayed in his state of trancelike meditation for almost
two hours, then abruptly his body speeded up to a normal rate

and he became aware of his surroundings. A course of action had been decided.

Socrates went down to the equipment locker and removed a nylon rope and a pair of double-sheave pulleys. He threaded the rope through the pulleys and carefully placed the apparatus at the side of the docking-mechanism airlock. Returning to the control room, he donned his lifesuit, sealed the helmet, and went on to internal life support. Then he evacuated the atmosphere from inside *Odysseus*. He lined the ship with the dock once again, and applied minimum thrust in the shortest pulse he could manage. Ship and station were now about fifty meters apart.

Socrates went to the ship's docking hatch and opened it to space. Tying one of the pulleys to the inner handrail, he pulled himself out through the hatch. Then he reached back in and pulled the other pulley out with him. He wedged his feet around the two outer handrails and stood in the lock, watching as the two docks closed and the space station slowly blotted out the sky over his head.

Slowly, ever so slowly, the docks came together, and Socrates could see that they were slightly out of line. Something had thrown the ship slightly off course, and the mating was not going to be perfect. There wouldn't be enough time for Socrates to get back to the pilot's seat, apply correction, and make it back down to the hatch. He'd just have to hope that the drift wouldn't be so bad that he couldn't manually compensate—by physically pulling the two hatches together and forcing them to mate.

It wouldn't be easy. Even in weightless space mass was still a problem. The mass of *Odysseus* was about half that of a destroyer, and the space station would have made a good cruiser. If the two came together wrong, with Socrates between, they could crush him to a pulp or shear him neatly in half without severely affecting the momentum of either.

Socrates's helmet was now surrounded by the station's locking ring. Slowly it approached its mate and swallowed Socrates. Then the lip of the ring cut off the sun and his head went into the shadow. It was completely black, and he had forgotten to bring a torch. There was no way to go back for one now.

Socrates pulled himself forward, his arms outstretched, until his right hand reached the station's airlock. He felt around the exterior of the airlock until he found the inset wheel that opened it. Bracing himself as best he could with his free left hand, he twisted the wheel. At first it didn't want to move, but then it broke free and smoothly slid around a half turn and clicked open. The lock opened in and Socrates pushed at it until it was wide open.

The ship and the station were now pressed lock to lock, but again they had not mated. They were not perfectly aligned, but the six or eight centimeters they were away from perfection should have been self-correcting and they should have just slid together. This was not happening. With a low, grinding noise *Odysseus* pressed more firmly against *Quetzalcoatl* and the two locks scraped metal across metal and prepared to part.

Socrates tossed the free end of the rope through the gap and then followed it through the lock and into the station. He felt around the smooth metal tube that was the inside of the airlock for the handrails and tied the second tackle to the farthest one he could find. Then he pulled on the free rope until he had taken up the slack between the two tackles. He looped the rope around one of the handrails and, twisting himself around until he could plant his feet against the inner lock door, pulled the rope tight.

His arm and shoulder muscles, kept in shape on the springs and torsion bars of the ship's no-gravity gym, pulled slowly and evenly against their new load, gradually increasing the tension. The rope pulled taut, stretched, and held. And would go no further. And then, so slowly that at first he wasn't sure that it wasn't his imagination, the rope pulled out again.

Quickly Socrates took a hitch around the handrail and tied off the rope. Over a period of minutes it stretched out and pulled cable-taut, and the pulleys creaked, the sound transmitted through the walls of the airlock into his suit, and time was a function of the elasticity of the nylon rope. Then the pulley stopped creaking and the only sound was Socrates breathing in his helmet. He kept a hand on the rope to feel the tension, and cursed his forgetfulness and the lack of a torch. His hand, through the heavy space mitten, could detect no change.

Then the pulley creaked again and the tension on the rope eased the slightest bit. The ships were no longer being pulled apart.

Socrates pulled the hitch loose and once more tried pulling up on the rope. With his legs and back braced and all his muscles tensed, he could just detect the slightest, barely perceptible motion of the rope. The nylon had held, and its elasticity had been enough to take up the energy moving the ships apart and start them together again. Socrates kept up his steady pull on the rope, although whether he was actually helping he couldn't tell.

The ships came together, pressed lock to lock, and there was a thumping and then a clicking sound transmitted through the suit, and *Odysseus* was docked.

Socrates relaxed in the cramped lock for a long minute, using a meditation exercise he had been trained in, and then opened the inner lock and entered the station.

〰〰〰〰〰〰〰

19

The Simples dressed in tunics of unbleached homespun; some trimmed in badly tanned leather, some in bits of ancient drapery or rug. They wore thonged sandals or boots, and all who were otherwise unarmed carried six-foot staves. Mordecai and company, after leaving the Western Division of Nebraska's militia behind at Lexington, ran into their first examples of the Simple Horde outside of Grand Island.

A log fortification, consisting of several logs one atop the other, had been erected by the side of the road. Several Simples crouched behind this breastwork and trained crossbows on the horses and on Mordecai, their driver. Several others, carrying twelve-foot lances, stood out in the middle of the road, lances lowered, and blocked the way.

"Hold that rig, good sir," the lanceman on the left requested.

Mordecai pulled to a stop. "Is this some sort of brigandage?" he demanded. "If so, we are but poor traveling pilgrims and have nothing of interest to robbers. Except, perhaps, a few crusts of poor, stale bread which we would be willing to share with anyone in need."

"We will take nothing from thee, good sir," the Simple scout said. "Thou are Mordecai, the magician?"

"I am known as Mordecai," Mordecai said cautiously.

"Thou will accompany us, please," the Simple said.

"Where are we going?" Mordecai asked.

The Simple stood for a moment, silently considering. "All will become known to thee," he said finally. "Thine is not to reason why." Then he backed off and came to a position of Present Lance. Then he went to Port Lance, to Order Lance, to Trail Lance, and then at ease. It looked very showy and professional in an insane sort of way, but gave no further information about what was going on.

Ruth parted the canvas in front of the wagon and emerged to sit next to Mordecai on the driver's bench. "What do they want with us?" she asked.

"They were expecting us," Mordecai said. "I have no idea what that means. They're going to escort us somewhere when they get around to it. Just hold tight and look unconcerned."

"The quality of advice you give me gets more and more strained," Ruth told Mordecai, smiling sweetly up at him before disappearing back into the wagon.

After about half an hour their escort arrived, in the form of a troop of Simple cavalry with crossbows slung over the backs of their leather jackets, short swords at their waists, and wide, bristly mustaches. The whole troop sported glossy black derby hats, worn flat on their heads. Most of them had long single braids coming out straight back from under the hat.

The troop took positions around Mordecai's wagon like the cavalry guarding the settlers, and their leader came up to Mordecai and raised a clenched fist with index and pinky fingers extended. "In the name of Brother Simon I greet thee," he said. "Do not overtax thy horses; Brother Simon understands human frailty. Shall we begin?"

"Where are we going?" Mordecai asked.

"To greet Brother Simon," the leader said. "Thou may prod thy horses into motion any time now."

They traveled for about a day and a half under the close escort of Brother Simon's Riders before reaching Lincoln. The horsemen stayed a proper and respectful distance away at all times. Dealing with a magician was clearly not within the scope of their general orders. Mordecai tried to get some basic information from them, such as where they had heard of him and why they were going wherever they were going, but the art of speech deserted them whenever they approached him.

Lincoln, Nebraska, had burned to the ground at least fifty years ago. On the ashes of the old Lincoln a new Lincoln, smaller, rougher-hewed, had grown. This too, now, had burned, was burning still in places. The stone wall surrounding the new Lincoln, constructed of the bricks and stones of the old Lincoln, was breached in several places and surrounded by rubble. A few stone buildings inside the wall were still standing, but little else was.

Outside the wall a slapdash tent city was being thrown up by the survivors. Few of the tents would have won merit badges for construction. They were made from sacks, rugs, bedspreads, drapes, bolts of cloth, and whatever else had been salvaged; and their motley appearance gave the area a look of bizarre, almost insane gaiety, like a hobo carnival.

"You may wait here," the leader of the cavalry troop said, waving a gloved hand toward the edge of the tent city. "You will be called."

"I'm sure," Mordecai said.

The troop rode off, leaving two of their number to wait and watch at a respectful distance, and make sure that Mordecai stayed until called.

Peter guided the wagon over to a clear space by the tent city and the three of them fastened it down and staked out the horses. The people in the makeshift tents kept about their own business and paid no attention to the newcomers; but then they paid very little attention to each other. Small children toddled in the direction of the strange wagon, but they were retrieved or removed as soon as an adult noticed their aberrant behavior.

It was Ruth's turn to cook dinner, and she set about constructing a small fire out of their store of dried kindling; anything burnable in their immediate area had already been burned.

Ruth set the tripod grate over her small fire and put the heavy pot on the grate. In the pot she created a stew; a process she had become quite proficient at. Mordecai paused to sniff at the boiling stock. "It never ceases to amaze me," he told her, "that all three of us create the same monotonous meal out of the same invariable ingredients, yet when you do it the resulting concoction tastes better. How do you explain that?"

Ruth stood up, brushed the hair away from her eyes, and glared at him. "It's called 'male chauvinism,'" she said, clutching the ladle in an unfeminine manner in her right hand.

"Oh," Mordecai said mildly, "is that what it is?"

"According to the map," Peter said, appearing from behind the wagon, "the Lincoln enclave should be a few miles north of here along this road. That is, if it hasn't been burned to the ground. We going to try and contact them?"

"We'll play it by ear," Mordecai said, drawing random patterns in the earth with his staff. "We must distribute our biological supplies over as wide an area as possible; but there's little use in leaving a kit with the survivors if the enclave's been destroyed. They'll have neither the time nor the facilities to do anything with it, nor the interest to try."

Ruth ladled the stew into three bowls. "What about the letter?" she asked. "The one you're supposed to deliver here."

"The temptation is to burn it now, and bury the ashes," Mordecai said. "The address is surely burned. But the man may not be—and I gave my word." He stared off into space for a minute, then tapped his staff firmly on the hard earth. "We shall try to find the gentleman," he said. "But not at the risk of our own mission. These Simples aren't complete fools; or at least we can't assume they are without further proof. So we look for the gentleman subtly. If we find him we deliver his mail; if not, it goes into the dead-letter office."

"What's his name?" Peter asked.

"What do you suppose the Simples brought us here for?" Ruth asked.

"R. B. (Bob) Patterson is his name, and I don't know, in that order," Mordecai said. "They seem obsessed with the idea that I'm a magician. That's why I've started carrying this staff: it's good for the image."

"I thought you were feeling your age," Ruth said, smiling sweetly.

"Arby Bob?" Peter asked. "What sort of name is that?"

"That's R period, B period, parentheses Bob, end parentheses, Patterson; and it's some sort of ritualistic Midwestern name."

"What's in the letter anyway?" Peter asked. "What's so important that we have to risk our lives lugging it through enemy lines?"

"Don't be overly dramatic," Mordecai told him. "We're not at war with anyone, and our personal preference in this dispute is our own business. There's almost no risk in taking a letter that looks like an innocuous request for goods among a group of peo-

ple who can't read anyhow. They're just as likely to hang us for
having a book as for having a letter of any sort."

They broke off their conversation as a man approached the fire,
and they silently watched him draw near. He was tall and muscu-
lar, clean-shaven, balding except for a thin horseshoe of hair, and
he wore a plain brown robe tied with a knotted length of rope.
"Good evening," he said when he was close enough to be heard
without raising his voice. "You are Mordecai?"

Mordecai stood, leaning against his staff, and nodded. "My
fame seems to precede me. I am he. What can I do for you?"

"I welcome you to Lincoln, or what used to be Lincoln until
the day before yesterday. And your assistants, of course. I am Friar
Randall, a lay brother of the Nebraska Universalist Eclectic Institute, which used to be known as the University of Nebraska at
Lincoln, and is now simply called the enclave. I would that it could
be a better welcome, but the Simples have removed from us the
ability to observe the formalities."

"Ah, Friar Randall," Mordecai said, taking his hand. "Come
join us. Have some stew. You were expecting us?"

"There are brothers watching every entrance to town," Friar
Randall told them. "We had a description of you, and what you
carry, on our radio about a month ago. The timing was good,
as our radio broke down a few days later and none of us has been
able to get it in operation again. It hums, sometimes it whistles;
but it no longer speaks."

Ruth ladled Friar Randall a bowl of soup, which he accepted
gratefully. "I did not care to ask the townspeople to feed me," he
said. "They are wondering why the Simples burned them out but
didn't touch the enclave. As a result, the long and happy relationship between town and robe in this area would appear to be over."

"Then the enclave is unharmed?" Mordecai asked.

Friar Randall shrugged. "It's a matter of definition," he said.
"Our buildings were not burned, our men were not slaughtered,
our women were not raped. In that way we are better off than the
town. So far. But the town has had its tragedy, and will now be
free to rebuild. They will have to pay lip service to the philosophy
of Brother Simon and the Simples, but they will be otherwise left
alone."

"And the enclave?" Mordecai asked.

"I thought that Brother Simon was antiscience," Peter said. "How come you weren't burned along with the town?"

"Ah!" Friar Randall said, squatting before the small fire. "A very wise president of the university, many years ago, saw what he believed to be a wave of antiscientific feeling sweeping through the survivors of the Death. He changed the name of the university and put us all, students and faculty, in these brown robes. We are ascetic holy men, us: historians and scholars of the Bible. We may dabble in biology, and do a little physics on the side, but it's for internal consumption only. Protective camouflage, you might say."

"But Brother Simon isn't going to leave you to your quiet biblical studies?" Mordecai asked.

"That is so," Friar Randall agreed. "This time our cover backfired on us, to mix a metaphor. Brother Simon desires us biblical scholars to find the precise spot in the Holy Book which foretells his coming. He earnestly desires this. We have a month."

Mordecai nodded thoughtfully. "I can see that your way is fraught with difficulty," he said.

"Is he serious?" Peter asked.

"Brother Simon? He is at least very earnest," Friar Randall said. "However this is all our problem. I believe you have a package for us?"

"Some, ah, biblical material," Mordecai agreed. "From Revelations mostly. A little glassware and a little cookbook. Now let's hope that we can get you the required spice."

"Thyme, I suppose," Friar Randall said. "Martian thyme. A time to live and a time to die." He stared into the fire. " 'The bird of time has but a little way to flutter . . .' but I digress."

"Any word from Mars?" Mordecai asked. "We've been on the road."

"Sorry," Friar Randall said. "As I mentioned, our radio has been whistling. We have neither the equipment nor the knowledge to repair those little chips. We tried blowing a couple of glass tubes —diodes—and winding coils and the like, but we can't even get a whistle out of our homemade rig. If you run across an itinerant electronic engineer who'd like to be a monk for a while, send him around."

"You have my word," Mordecai said. "Are you ready to take your package now?"

"If it's small enough for one man to carry conveniently and inconspicuously, I am. What do we have to do to prepare; and how will we get the serum or vaccine or whatever it is?"

"Breed some convenient laboratory animal. Rabbits are probably best. It's all in the book. As to when and how, I wish I could tell you. Someone will be back. If there's any reason to come back. If you haven't heard in, say, six months . . ."

Friar Randall waited silently for a moment, until he realized that Mordecai wasn't going to complete his thought. Then he nodded slowly. "I shall so inform the lay brethren," he said.

Mordecai climbed into the wagon and came back out with a small sack. "Here's the book," he said, "and a few sample pieces of equipment for you to duplicate. If you can blow diodes, you should have little trouble with this glassware. Good luck."

"The diodes didn't work," Friar Randall said, staring at the sack. Then he took it and shook Mordecai's hand firmly, and then Ruth's, and then Peter's. "Go with God," he said.

"Would you like to sleep in the shelter of our wagon tonight, and return to the enclave in the morning?" Mordecai asked. "The sun is down, and it will be dark within half an hour."

"I prefer to travel after dark," Friar Randall said. "For an unsuperstitious traveler who knows the road, dark is indeed the best time to travel these days. I won't ask you to stop in at the institute, as we're turning away all travelers and wouldn't want to draw attention to either of us by making an exception of you. But if you return this way you must be our guests. *Au revoir.*"

Friar Randall turned and, without looking back, headed off down the road.

Early the next morning the mounted troops returned for them. "Get those horses hitched, magician," the troop leader yelled from a safe distance. "Brother Simon wants you." And he fidgeted impatiently on his horse until the wagon was ready to move.

They went around the ruined city by a road that moved alongside the wall. The road was now covered with battle rubble to such an extent that Peter had to get down from the wagon several times and lead the horses around the piles of stone or half-burned timber. Twice they all had to dismount and clear away the road until the wagon could pass. Their mounted escort watched all this closely but made no move to help.

On the far side of Lincoln they came to a great encampment of Simples. A large white tent took up the central area of the encampment, with a great parade ground cleared in front of it. As they approached, a group of Simple horsemen were riding back and forth on the parade ground, hacking at each other with wooden swords. It seemed to be a complete free-for-all, with no sides and no rules. Periodically one of the horsemen would throw his arms back and fall off his horse, then jump back on and barge into the fight again. Once in a while someone would slump off his horse and fall down, and not get up; but usually he would be dragged off the field before he was trampled. All in all, it looked like good, clean, simple-minded fun.

Their escort brought them to the side of the white tent and told them to wait. At first it looked as though they were being completely ignored, but it soon became evident that the Simples in camp were very deliberately refusing to look at them or acknowledge their existence.

"Again, I fear, our fame has spread before us," Mordecai said. "These people are afraid of us. They've been warned that a magician is coming to camp."

"We're even," Peter said. "I'm afraid of them."

A tall man in white robes came out of the white tent carrying a large brass gong. A shorter man in white robes followed him out, carrying a mallet. They both stopped and faced each other. The tall one held the gong out on a wooden handle. The shorter one struck it with the mallet, and the sound reverberated over the field. Everyone instantly stopped what they were doing and turned to look at the white tent. The gong was struck again, and the Simples ran to positions in front of the tent and dropped to their knees.

The tent flaps were pushed back and two more men in white robes came out carrying slide trombones. They took up positions on either side of the flaps and raised their instruments to their lips. A second pair with snare drums joined the slide trombonists.

Then, to the tune of "A Mighty Fortress is our God," as arranged for trombone and drum, a short man in blood-red robes with a red cowl shading his face strode out of the white tent. After ten paces he stopped and raised his hands in benediction over the kneeling Simples. He wore spotless white gloves.

The music stopped and the whole area grew deathly silent. Suddenly one of the trombonists yelled, "All down before Simon, the Scourge of God!"

"He is our brother!" the multitude yelled in return, and fell flat on their faces.

"Simon will cleanse and make us well," the trombonist yelled.

"Brother Simon!" the crowd returned.

"Simon will scour and keep us well."

"Brother Simon!"

"Keep us simple and healthy and well."

"Brother Simon!"

"We do for Simon, and he keeps us well."

"We do!" the crowd yelled. "We do! We do! We do!"

"I wonder what they do," Peter whispered to Mordecai.

"Let's hope we never find out," Mordecai whispered in reply.

Brother Simon, the Scourge of God, put his hands down to his sides and stared at his people. "Thou are simple," he called in a high voice that didn't carry very well. But his people knew the litany.

"We are simple," they yelled.

"Thou are pure."

"We are pure."

"Thou are well."

"And Simon is our brother."

"It is mercy . . ." Simon called.

". . . to do for Simon," his people finished.

"It is justice . . ."

". . . to do for Simon. We do! We do! We do!"

Simon raised his arms again. "I am thy brother," he called.

The crowd went wild with screaming and clapping for almost two minutes. Then, as though at some prearranged signal that Mordecai and company didn't catch, they suddenly stopped and were silent.

Simon turned on his heel and strode back into his tent. As he disappeared through the flap, the mob outside broke up to resume whatever activity they had stopped five minutes before.

About two minutes later a white-robed minion came out of the tent and cautiously approached Mordecai. "Are thou the magician?" he asked.

Mordecai nodded assent.

"Will thou please follow me," he said, lifting the hem of his robe and turning back to the tent.

Mordecai leaned back. "Stay here," he instructed Ruth and Peter, "unless they tell you to move. Then do it without arguing. Look cool and relaxed and answer no questions. If you don't hear from or about me by nightfall, each of you take a horse and head for Chicago. Leave the wagon. 'Bye now." And he climbed off his seat on the wagon and, staff firmly in hand, strode after the man in white.

The white tent was quite large inside. It was floored by an overlapping series of oriental rugs that, if Mordecai was any judge, occupied the walls of some museum before covering the dirt of this Nebraska field. A long, low table straddled the center of the tent area, effectively dividing it into two. The back half had several canvas chairs, several large cushions, and a scattering of large trunks of assorted types, like the loot of some ancient luggage shop. The front half held but four guards, frozen into formal postures of attention.

Brother Simon and about ten high-ranking Simples were gathered around the central table, to which was pinned a large road map of the Free State of Nebraska. Brother Simon stood at the center of the group, impressively silent, brooding, staring down at the map. His staff argued, gesticulated, pounded the table, drew heavy lines on the map with various implements, and one little man periodically hopped on one foot and then the other.

Mordecai's escort took him over to one side of the tent, obviously waiting for the proper moment to present him to Brother Simon. Mordecai made use of the time to study the man who had gone to so much trouble to meet him.

Brother Simon was a short, stocky man with a barrel chest and unnaturally long arms. His hands were still covered by the spotless white gloves. His head, no longer hidden by the cowl, seemed too large for his body; with a great, hawklike nose, and deep-set, brooding eyes under heavy brows. His long brown hair was combed straight back and fell below his shoulders. He was clean-shaven.

Simon seemed to possess the ability to focus his attention to-tally on whatever was at hand. Right now he was studying the map and plotting his battle strategy for the next day, and nothing else existed for him. If the tent had caught fire, he would not have no-ticed until a burning piece of canvas fell on the map, or the smoke obscured his vision.

"Where is my Ninth?" Brother Simon asked.

"Here," one of his staff pointed to a spot on the map.

"Hmmm. And the mounted Fourth?"

"Last we heard, which was yesterday evening, they'd cut a salient about as far as, um, here."

"No word today?"

"None."

"Hmmm," Simon said. "Any reason to assume they didn't make it through to Norfolk?"

"None."

"Then we must assume they did." His gloved hand roamed over the map while he thought. "The Nebraskans are clearly going to defend Omaha. Which clearly means that we will have Omaha surrounded, effectively surrounded, by the end of the week."

"We can be ready to attack Omaha by Tuesday," an aide told him.

"No," Simon said, waving a gloved finger. "We will make them come to us. If we have Omaha surrounded, the body of Nebraska's army to the west must come to their relief. And that army we shall destroy. After that we can take Omaha at our leisure. We must get our reserve up from Kansas City, and prepare for a decisive battle somewhere west of Omaha. Draw up the necessary orders." This last was directed to a man who sat at one corner of the table with pen and paper at the ready, and he immediately started scratching the pen across the paper.

Brother Simon looked up. "Is there anything else?"

"There's the matter of grain for the troops, Brother," an aide reminded him.

"True," he said. "Send foraging parties a day's ride to the, um" —he stared at the map—"south. Tell the sergeants to offer the farmers our usual terms: four sacks of grain and we don't burn their barns and houses, six sacks and we don't molest their women or children. But make sure to give them all official receipts for everything requisitioned."

"But most of the sergeants don't know how to write."

"That doesn't matter: most of the farmers don't know how to read," Brother Simon said. "Now move thy ass."

"Very good, Brother," the aide said. He raised his fist with the pinky and forefinger extended. "I do for Simon," he said, and backed out of the tent.

"Yes," Simon said. Then he noticed Mordecai. "Ah!" he said. "Thou must be the magician, Mordecai."

"I must," Mordecai agreed.

"Come forward, magician," Simon said. "Are thou truly a magician?"

Mordecai had been expecting that question for some time now, and had worked out several possible answers to it, depending on circumstances. However, these circumstances still gave him no clue as to what Brother Simon had in mind. "Yes," he said.

"I have heard reports of thy power. Thou can make people float?" Brother Simon came around the table and stopped a respectful distance away from Mordecai. "In air, I mean."

"Sometimes," Mordecai said cautiously.

Brother Simon backed up to the table, still staring at Mordecai, and sat on its edge. "Do something," he directed, gesturing vaguely into the air.

Mordecai nodded and, meeting Brother Simon's stare with a firm, unyielding gaze, stretched his staff out in front of him, holding it at arm's length with both hands. Then he ran his hands along the staff until they met at the balance point, and took his right hand away, lowering the arm to his side. The staff was now balanced horizontally in his left hand. Slowly he opened the hand, palm down, fingers wide; and the staff *did not fall*. He raised the hand a few inches and the staff floated there.

There was a sharp intake of breath from the dozen or so people in the tent as they watched the six-foot wooden staff swaying slightly, unsupported, four feet in the air.

"Witch!" one of the men gasped, almost involuntarily.

The staff thumped to the rug and Mordecai dropped his arm. "Who said that?" he asked, bending over to pick up the staff, his gaze darting from one to the other of Brother Simon's aides. "You have broken the spell."

The aide stepped forward defiantly. "Are thou not a witch?" he demanded.

Mordecai glared at him. "No, sir," he said sharply. "I am a magician. I can read the Bible clearly and loudly, as you know no witch can. As a matter of fact," he added, fixing the man with his stare, "there are a few of the passages that I can read more clearly than you, and with a clearer conscience."

"Thou are a magician," Brother Simon acknowledged. He turned to the rest of his aides. "Get out," he said. "You too," he told the guards. "Leave us alone. Stay right outside the tent. I'll call you back."

There was no argument, and in a minute the tent was empty of all save Brother Simon and Mordecai. "Come," Simon said, walking over to the rear of the table. "I have something to ask of thee." He poured wine from a crystal carafe into two silver goblets and handed one of them to Mordecai.

"I will do what is within my power to aid a mighty prince such as yourself," Mordecai said diplomatically. "But battles cannot be won by magic, and he who tells you otherwise is a knave."

"Bah!" Brother Simon said. "I need no man's help in winning battles. I am a natural tactical genius, like Napoleon, Hitler, and Custer. Besides, I know something of the power of magic: I was raised in Pennsylvania."

"I see," Mordecai said.

"I may trust thee?" Brother Simon asked. "I know I cannot compel a magician with physical force; the spells don't work then. But if thou betray me, I can get thee."

Mordecai mupped himself up to his tallest and looked offended. "Have I not taken the Mantic Oath?" he demanded. "Am I not a licensed thaumaturge, sworn to Saint Gregory? Whatever secrets you entrust with me could not be torn out of me by fire."

"Calm down," Brother Simon said, refilling Mordecai's goblet. "I did not mean to insult thee. Thou have answered my question. Now, what is thy fee for a small, hmm, hexerei, and how long will it take, and what will thou require?"

"The fee is whatever you think it's worth," Mordecai said. "In silver, of course, as is traditional. As to the rest, I'll have to know what the job is first."

"Yes," Brother Simon said, looking embarrassed. He took a deep breath and then pulled off the white glove on his right hand. "It's this," he said, thrusting the hand out at Mordecai for examination and looking away. The hand was small, with stubby fingers, and the back of it was covered with a cluster of great warts, like toadstools thrust up overnight on a lawn.

"I see," Mordecai said. "And the other one?"

"The same," Brother Simon said. "Since two years now. And getting worse."

"Anywhere else?" Mordecai asked.

"Yes," Brother Simon said, but without amplification.

"I see," Mordecai repeated. "You want them removed?"

Brother Simon picked the glove off the table and thrust his hand back into it. "Is it not a common hexerei?" he demanded.

"It is," Mordecai agreed. "I will need a day to prepare. Tomorrow at noon, or shortly thereafter, I shall perform a simple rite. Within a week they will start to recede. Within two weeks they will be gone. My assistants and I must have complete freedom of the countryside this evening to pick certain herbs and—other things—after dark."

"Agreed." He walked Mordecai to the tent flap and told a runner, who ran to tell Mordecai's escort, that Mordecai and associates were to have free run of the countryside.

"Until tomorrow," Mordecai said, raising his staff in benediction.

Peter stayed to mind the wagon while Mordecai and Ruth rode off into the dusk. They had decided that, in the interest of mobility and unobtrusiveness, it would be wise to saddle two of the horses rather than drag the wagon around behind them. Besides, keeping the wagon in camp would reassure Brother Simon that Mordecai wasn't planning to run out before next day's ceremony. And keeping Peter on the wagon would restrain the natural urge to search it if it was left empty. Simon wouldn't want to offend someone who was to perform cosmetic magic for him the next day.

The address of R. B. (Bob) Patterson was outside of the walled city, and quite possibly beyond the radius of destruction. There

was, of course, the question of whether R. B. (Bob) himself had
been spared along with his house, but they would soon find out.
Mordecai would either deliver the letter or burn it by the end of
that evening.

They paused periodically along the road and searched out random leaves or flowers with an intentness of purpose that would
have convinced any observer. When the last gleam of daylight had
disappeared in the west, Mordecai and Ruth headed directly for
the Patterson house. No one, Mordecai was prepared to believe,
was going to attempt to follow a magician at night.

The house was still standing and looked, as best they could tell
at night, untouched. A tall barn or silo or something rose behind
it, blotting out the stars.

They tied their horses to the picket fence and crossed the yard.
A soft light was coming from one of the front windows, probably
a candle or oil lamp, but they couldn't see or hear any motion from
inside. Mordecai knocked on the door. After a pause he pounded
on the door.

Soft footsteps sounded from inside, and the door opened. A
small, ancient lady stood in the doorway, wrapped in a quilted
robe, with a cotton nightcap on her head and thick cotton slip-
pers. "He's not home," she said.

"Who isn't home?" Mordecai asked.

"Who else?" she responded. "Nobody comes by at this time of
night to see me."

"We'd like to speak to Mr. Patterson," Ruth said. "Mr. R. B.
Patterson."

"That's R. B. (Bob)," the old lady said. "And he still isn't
home." She looked Ruth up and down, stared at the riding pants
Ruth was wearing, and sniffed.

"I have an important letter for him," Mordecai said.

"I'll give it to him," the old lady said. "Hand it over." She stuck
out a gnarled hand.

"I must hand it to him personally," Mordecai said. "You don't
know where we could find him?"

"Listen, lady," Ruth said, "we're friends of his. It's very important that we find him tonight. We may not have a chance to come
back."

"You a friend of his, are you?" the woman said, staring suspiciously at Ruth. "I'm his mother, and I've never seen you here before. R. B. (Bob) wouldn't run off to see no lady friends behind my back."

"I'm not a lady friend," Ruth said, trying not to let her exasperation show. "I'm a business friend, you might say."

"What business is that?" the old lady sniffed.

Ruth was feeling a personal commitment to get that letter delivered; a feeling that had been growing the more time she spent among the Simples. And Mordecai, by all the signs she'd learned to recognize, considered his promise kept with this attempt. She knew that Mordecai had sworn to deliver the letter only into Patterson's own hands, but surely his mother . . . But mother's suspicions and surliness weren't helping matters any.

Mordecai lifted his hat. "I'm sorry to have troubled you, madam," he said. "When R. B. (Bob) returns, please tell him that we dropped by. Mutual friends of Captain Mollet, you may say. And we're sorry to have missed him. Come along, Ruth."

"Captain Mollet, you say?" the old woman asked, stopping Mordecai in mid-turn.

He turned back. "That is correct, madam. Captain Mollet."

"Come in," the old lady said, standing aside. "Don't stand in the doorway like that. Whyn't you say so before?" She ushered them into the front room, sat them on a creaky horsehair sofa, and disappeared into the rear of the house.

"Sorry about that," she said, appearing a minute later. "I thought you were some of them Simple bastards. My son'll be along in a minute. You just caught him. He was fixing to leave in a minute."

"Hello there," a short, bald man said, coming into the room. "Would you like a cool drink? Ma, fix them up with a cool drink. A couple of glasses of grape juice would be nice."

"Of course," the old lady said. "How thoughtless of me. Be right back." And she disappeared into the rear of the house again.

"My name is R. B. (Bob) Patterson," the short man said, leaning up against the door jamb. He was dressed in dark pants and a dark jacket, with many pockets, that went down almost to his knees. He kept his right hand in one of the pockets. "I understand you have a letter for me from Captain Mollet."

Mordecai produced the letter without a word and handed it to Patterson. Slitting open the seals of the envelope with his left thumb, Patterson shook the letter out, allowing the envelope to flutter to the floor. He moved over to the one lamp in the room, a kerosene lamp with a glass chimney sitting on the table by the wall, and read the letter; his eyes shifted constantly between the paper and Mordecai and Ruth. When he was about halfway down the page he abandoned his attempt to keep his two guests in sight and concentrated fully on the letter.

"Fascinating," Patterson said finally, putting the letter on the table. He took his right hand out of his jacket pocket, producing a large, cocked revolver, which he put on half-cock and thrust in his belt.

"You're a suspicious man," Mordecai said.

"The Simples have put a price on my head," Patterson said.

"So," Mordecai said. "Then why haven't they been here before this?"

"They don't know it's me they're after," Patterson explained. "Although they undoubtedly will any day now. I was just getting ready to leave, as it happens."

"Excuse me, but, what do you mean: they don't know it's you they're after?" Ruth asked.

"Grape juice!" Patterson's mother said, coming back in with a tray with four glasses. She handed them around.

Patterson drained his glass in one tilt, and put it down. "The Simples know only my working name," he said. "The name under which I've organized a string of agents all over their territory who keep track of their movements and report directly to me."

"Spies!" Ruth said.

"Then you must be used to people coming by and knocking on your door in the middle of the night," Mordecai said.

"Oh, no," Patterson said. "I could never allow that. It would be too dangerous. Besides, my mother needs her sleep."

"Then how do you communicate?" Mordecai asked.

"By air," Patterson said.

"Air?"

"Pigeons. Classic in its simplicity. We lose a few to hawks every month, but over eighty per cent get through."

"And the Simples haven't tumbled to this?" Mordecai asked.

"They seem to be innocent of the habits of nesting doves," Patterson said. "One day, I suppose, a Simple trooper will shoot one down for breakfast and notice the message on its leg, then we'll be blown. Then, of course, they'll all go crazy thinking every bird they see is a secret messenger. It might almost be worth it."

"What is your working name?" Ruth asked, obviously fascinated at meeting a real live spy.

Patterson smiled shyly. "Pieman," he said. "They call me Pieman."

Mordecai broke out laughing, and after a second Patterson joined him. Ruth considered this for a minute and managed a smile. Mrs. Patterson scowled. "You'd think when a body's risking his life, day after day," she said, "he'd learn to take things seriously. You'd think so," she said, "wouldn't you?" She sniffed. "I'll be in my room. I've said good-bye." She paused in the doorway for a moment and then left the room.

"You're going?" Mordecai asked.

Patterson nodded. "West," he said. "My pigeons and I. We can't stay here any longer. The Simples are getting anxious, and close."

"The roads are closely watched," Mordecai said. "People are coming in, but nobody is leaving. The people of Lincoln are camping outside the gates of their burned town because they can't get away. How are you going to get through the lines?"

"By air," Patterson said.

"Air?"

"Come with me," Patterson said. "I'll show you." He led them out the back of the house to the structure they had thought to be a silo or barn when they saw it looming over the house from the road. It was neither silo nor barn.

It was black, and round, and six stories high, and tied down with ropes. At its base was a large wicker basket full of wicker cages full of birds.

"A balloon!" Ruth said.

Mordecai stared up at the giant orb of black fabric blotting out the night sky. "Magnificent!" he said. "Hydrogen?"

"I'm not so technically minded," Patterson said. "Hot air's the best I can manage." He showed Mordecai the twin burners and the kerosene tanks. "Got enough fuel for four or five hours, I figure," he said. "By that time, if the east wind holds up, I'll be comfortably into the Nebraska Free State. Well, I'd best get going. Would you cast off for me?"

Patterson climbed into the wicker basket, and Ruth and Mordecai went around loosing the ropes that held him down. There were twelve of them, and as the last one was pulled loose the six-story globe bobbed upward, impatient to be free. It rose steadily and, at about a hundred feet, caught a strong air current and moved purposefully off to the west.

Ruth and Mordecai stood staring after it until they could no longer make out its location even by the stars it occluded, then they turned and went back to the road.

~~~~~~~~~~~~~

20

The concrete runway at Chicago Spaceport was close to eight miles long and just about three miles wide. In the seventy-plus years it had been unused and untended, the fifteen thousand acres of flat, featureless concrete had remained unmarked, uncracked, and unweathered. Except for the layer of dirt and dust that formed wave patterns over the surface, it was as it had been. NASA had built for the ages, and the ages had passed. Not as planned, but they had passed.

Chicago Enclave had taken upon itself the responsibility for protecting the complex of buildings at the west end of the vast field; not as much from the ravages of time as from the attentions of passers-by: looters, crazies, vandals, and those good citizens whom the Lord had told to burn everything older than they were. Over the decades this had indeed been a responsibility. Chicago Spaceport, located just off route 80, immediately north and west of Ottawa, Illinois, was roughly eighty miles from the main buildings of Chicago Enclave, on the shores of Lake Michigan. The trip, which took two hours when they started taking it, now took two days. The guard, formerly mounted every day, was now on a one-month tour. Sophomores thought of it as part of the necessary harassment before advancing to junior status; a meaningless ritualistic formality.

But those buildings, for which more than one enclave guard had given his life in the old days when looting was still a way of life, were the substance of man's link with his spacefaring past. And, such are the ways of fate, his hope for the possibility of a future. Without the apparatus stored in these buildings, untouched for seven decades, no shuttlecraft could hope to find

Chicago Spaceport and land safely. Taking off again was another matter altogether.

"We have an obligation," Dr. Pepperidge said, staring out at the concrete horizon and the teams of freshmen busily sweeping it off. "We have an obligation to a Martian."

"We have more of an obligation to every human on Earth," Professor Jerob told him. "That serum that our friend Socrates is carrying is more important than his life—or yours or mine. He knew the risk he took in getting here when he volunteered."

"The risk he's taking getting here is probably not as bad as the odds against his living more than two weeks if he cracks his helmet open and takes one breath of Earth air," Dr. Pepperidge said. "We have to get that shuttle back in orbit before his canned air runs out. And if that kerosene doesn't get here before he does, it might just as well never have left Canada."

"The tanker's supposed to land tomorrow," Jerob said. "That gives them two days to get it here over land. If there's any hitch, we can ask Socrates not to come down for a couple or three days. As long as he stays at the space station, there's no time pressure. And he could stay there a month or two if he had to."

"I'd hate to have to ask him to stay in orbit after he's ready to come down," Dr. Pepperidge said. "What would he think of us?"

"He'd think we're trying to keep him alive," Jerob said. "Come on! We've got three hundred people from six different enclaves out here. We've got probably another three hundred working on this project around the country. We've got a tanker ship full of kerosene crossing Lake Michigan. We've got the liquid-oxygen plant downstairs running—sort of—for the first time since the Death. We've got groups all over the country ready to receive the serum when we get it and start growing the virus. We've got a wagon coming from California—California!—handing out cookbooks for virus culturing along the way.

"And as for our people here: we've figured out how to operate equipment nobody ever saw before, and got it in working order. We've got the radar working, and the approach control gizmo, and the landing lights, and the pumping stations, and the fire equipment—"

"The wheels on the fire trucks are all flat," Pepperidge said.

"They scoot along just fine on the rims," Jerob said. "Don't be a pessimist. We've had incredible luck, and done very well."

"It's the luck that scares me," Pepperidge said. He stared out the operations-room window. Outside, a tractor was pulling a huge, solid-fuel rocket across the field to the launch pad. It was the last of the cluster of three that would act as boosters to push the shuttle back up to space-station orbit. The other two were already in position. "Those rockets, for example. Supposing after all this time the solid propellant doesn't burn—or doesn't burn hot enough or long enough?"

"What has that to do with luck?" Jerob asked. "According to the best textbooks we can find, and our best reading of the specification manuals we've been able to find, the propellant should be stable for at least this long. If it isn't, we'll find out, won't we?"

"Sir!" a sophomore appeared at the operations-room door, leading a tall, skinny young man in ragged clothing. "A volunteer has just arrived. From New York Exclave. Robert Wail. And these gentlemen are Dr. Pepperidge and Professor Jerob; you'd best talk to them."

"Well," Pepperidge said heartily, letting this event break the spell of gloom he'd been surrounding himself with, "from the exclave, eh? We've been wondering why they didn't reply to our request for help."

"Excuse me, sir," Wail said. "I told them I was from the exclave, but I am not *of* the exclave. Not anymore."

"I have no idea what that means," Pepperidge said. "It sounds like a semantic quibble. Did any more of you exclave people come, or are you the entire delegation?"

"There is no delegation," Wail said. "That's what I'm trying to tell you. They're not planning to send anyone or offer any help. They think it's some kind of trick, at worst; or a waste of time at best. The deans and professors of the exclave are busy now cataloging and sorting their exhibits, so that if Homo sapiens is destroyed, they will at least leave an accurate museum of his history and accomplishments."

"For who?" Professor Jerob asked.

"Then what are you doing here?" Dr. Pepperidge asked.

"They kicked me out," Wail said. "I have been exiled; forbidden to set foot on the island of Manhattan again. So I came here, hoping there was some way I could help."

"I imagine we can put you to work," Jerob said.

"What did they kick you out for?" Pepperidge asked.

"I was a troublemaker."

"Well," Pepperidge said, "that's certainly direct. I don't know how much use we have for an avowed troublemaker here."

"What sort of trouble did you make?" Jerob asked.

"I wrote poetry," Wail said.

Jerob nodded. "The worst sort of troublemaker indeed. Well, I think we can find something for you to do. You don't know how to operate any kind of radio equipment, do you?"

"I've dusted off a few thousand radio sets in my freshman days," Wail said, "but I've never even seen one turned on."

"I thought not," Jerob said wistfully. "That's bad news you bring us about the exclave. We could have used their help. Or, if what you say is true, perhaps we couldn't. At any rate, we can certainly use yours. You have any outstanding skills—besides poetry? Anything you're particularly trained at or prepared for?"

"For the last year and a quarter I've been a cadet, sir," Wail said. "We all have to spend two years in the cadet corps. Kind of glorified guards. It's what I'm best at right now, although I don't like it very much. I can also catalog office copying machines of the twentieth century."

"We can use guards," Jerob said. "The natives are getting curious, and that's bad. Go report to the quartermaster in building B, and she'll assign you a bed. Then find the dean of guards and tell him of your previous experience. He'll probably make you a guard officer, since few of our boys have any kind of experience at all."

"Thank you," Wail said. "Thank you very much." He looked as if he was about to salute, then thought better of it and backed out of the door.

"What's this about curious natives?" Pepperidge asked. "You've been keeping things from me."

"I didn't want to worry you," Jerob said. "You have enough to worry about."

"Worry me," Pepperidge said.

"Our agents in the nearby towns; Ottawa and La Salle, and south to Streator—"

"What agents?" Pepperidge asked. "I didn't know we had agents."

"Mostly suppliers and day workers and the like," Jerob explained. "Some of them just sort of volunteer information over cups of tea, if you ask them right. Then they sort of get in the habit. I encouraged it; I thought it was a good idea. And I was right."

"Of course you were," Pepperidge agreed. "I never thought of it. You have an unexpectedly devious mind. I was never cut out for this sort of thing. I should have taught Einsteinian physics to graduate students and written papers on gravity fields for the journals. I have some original ideas on gravity fields. At least I think they're original. You know, if I'd been born a hundred and fifty years ago I might have been a Nobel Prize winner. I might. I was never cut out to be an administrator."

"You do fine," Jerob said. "Nobody likes your job, and nobody would be any more competent in it than you are. It has to be done."

"That's it," Pepperidge said, "cheer me up. And while you're at it, tell me more about these curious natives, and your spy apparat."

"My agents report increasing unrest in the towns," Jerob said. "Traveling preachers are coming in from all over and spreading the word that we're practicing science here again. Our grain suppliers are so worried that they've raised their prices. Claim it's dangerous to be seen driving a wagon here. We're going to start up the Death again, the rumor says. A couple of the real rabble-rousers are trying to get them worked up enough to come over here and burn everything down. They may succeed."

"It's wonderful how you know just what to say to cheer me up," Pepperidge said, staring glumly down at the endless expanse of concrete that was all that was visible through his window.

~~~~~~~~~~~~~~

21

Mordecai worked hard on preparations for his wart removal. "It's all in the preparation," he told Peter and Ruth. "If you believe warts are going to go away, then they usually go away. I have to make Brother Simon believe."

"I thought warts were caused by a virus," Peter said as he worked at chopping up a yellow plant Mordecai had brought back.

"Warts are very catholic," Mordecai said. "They are caused by a virus infection; they tend to appear during puberty, like acne; they favor the hands and feet; they spontaneously leave after being around for months—or years; they can be removed by chemicals or burning; they can also be removed by hypnotic suggestion. They offer a little something for every branch of medicine, from surgery to faith healing. And I'm not a surgeon."

When they had finished chopping up and mashing the plants Mordecai put them in an iron pot and set them to boil, seasoned with a couple of bottles of snake-oil elixir. "Aspirin," he said. "As the ancient saying goes, 'could it hurt?' "

"Has it occurred to you," Peter asked, "that Brother Simon will probably not want to let you out of his sight until his warts clear up?"

"I've been able to think of nothing else for the past few hours," Mordecai said. "However, I think I have devised a ploy; we shall see."

An hour later he lifted the lid of the pot and took a look at the brew. It was bubbling nicely, but there was no smell at all coming from the mixture. "Ruth!" he called. "Would you come here and smell this mess, please? I can't smell anything. Maybe it's just an old man's absent olfactory sense; there should be some odor with all that greenery we threw in."

Ruth came over and sniffed at the pot. "Lilac, I think," she said. "Just the faintest odor of lilac."

"That will never do," Mordecai said. "Everyone knows that magical concoctions have to smell obscene."

"What about that bison grease those men gave us?" Ruth asked. "That's the worst smell I've run across in some time."

"Do we still have it?" Mordecai asked.

"I put a coat of wax over the top to cut off the smell," Ruth said. "I'll get it." She went to the wagon and brought it out.

Mordecai broke the wax seal and smelled the grease. "Wow!" he said, quickly removing the jar from under his nose. "That's the stuff." With the aid of a stick, he pried most of the grease out and dumped it into the pot. Then he handed the jar to Ruth. "Dispose of that," he said. "Preferably underground and some distance from here."

"We'll probably have to throw the pot away, too," Ruth said. "We'll never get that smell out."

"I'll give it to Brother Simon as part of the treatment," Mordecai promised. "He deserves it." He let the mixture age for half an hour, then took it off the fire. Pulling a long, black cassock over his head, he belted it with a yellow rope and arranged the cowl over his head. "It's time," he said. "Pack up and get ready; we'll be leaving at dusk. I'll be back as soon as possible."

"You think they'll let us leave?" Peter asked sourly.

"I do," Mordecai said. "Trust the old man." He picked up his staff with his right hand and the pot, by a rag wrapped around the wire-loop handle, in his left, and strode toward the white tent.

The two guards at the door managed to convey extreme agitation beneath their frozen exteriors as Mordecai approached. They were obviously uncertain whether to bar the entrance or stand respectfully aside, clutching their lucky pieces. Mordecai simplified their problem by halting in front of the door. "I am expected," he told them. "Inform Brother Simon of my presence."

One of them ducked inside the tent to do so, while the other remained to stare worriedly at the weird old man carrying the iron pot.

It was Brother Simon himself who came to the door. "Magician," he said, "thou are prompt."

Mordecai strode by him and stopped at the center of the tent.

"First the cleansing ritual," he said, putting down the cast-iron pot and giving it three taps with the steel-shod end of his staff. "Please empty the tent of everyone but Brother Simon."

Simon's aides, gathered in the tent, looked eager to comply, but they all turned to Simon for the word. He nodded, and they all left the tent without quite running.

Mordecai had Simon stand in the middle of the tent, next to the iron pot. Then he drew a circle in the dirt around the inside of the tent wall, using the tip of his staff dipped in the gunk from the pot. He muttered old college-football fight songs and other incantations that came to mind as he spread the gunk.

That done, he returned to the center of the tent to face Brother Simon. "Remove your gloves," he commanded.

Brother Simon removed his gloves.

"Dip your hands into the potion," Mordecai ordered, "full up to the wrists."

"The smell—" Brother Simon began, his face wrinkled into an expression of intense dislike.

"I can do nothing about the smell," Mordecai said. "Dip!"

Brother Simon dipped.

"It is soothing," Mordecai said. "Soon the smell will not be noticed. Now anoint the other afflicted parts."

Brother Simon turned away from Mordecai and opened his robe. He took a gob of the greasy elixir in his right hand and spread it about his midsection. Then he took off his sandals and anointed his feet. "Done," he announced, standing up and re-fastening his robe. He turned back to Mordecai. "What now?"

"You must take neither food nor drink until sunset," Mordecai told him. "At that time you will appear before my wagon—alone. Bring as much silver as you can carry with one hand."

"The kettle?" Brother Simon asked as Mordecai began to leave without it.

"Leave it in place," Mordecai instructed him. "When the last wart has disappeared, bury it."

"Aha," Brother Simon said, nodding knowingly.

As the last rays of the sun winked out behind the western horizon, Brother Simon appeared before Mordecai's wagon, dressed all in white. No one else was in sight anywhere in the camp. "I am here," he said. "My hand is filled with silver." He carried a huge silver tea kettle with an ornately curved spout, holding it before him by the handle.

"So I see," Mordecai said, eyeing the tea kettle. "That isn't exactly what I had in mind, but I suppose it will do."

"Thou are getting the most silver I could carry with one hand," Brother Simon said. "This thing is damn heavy."

"No doubt," Mordecai said. "Your place is prepared; enter the wagon."

Brother Simon studied Mordecai's face for a minute. "Thou are not fool enough to try any hanky-panky with me, are thou? No, I guess not. I must have faith in someone, much as my troops have faith in me. And if thou can't trust a magician, who can thou trust?"

"Well put," Mordecai agreed. "Climb up."

Brother Simon handed the tea kettle up to Mordecai and then swung aboard. "My assistants," Mordecai said, indicating Peter and Ruth, who were sitting silently inside the wagon. "They will prepare you."

"Prepare me?" Brother Simon repeated doubtfully.

"Have faith," Mordecai said. "You will lay down on this pallet" —he indicated a pair of flat-top trunks pushed together—"on your back. The candles will be lighted, after which you will not speak until they are blown out. We will proceed very slowly along this road, going as close to due north as we can. Luckily, at this point the road goes basically north. After about half an hour we will stop. I shall speak further to you then." Mordecai climbed off the back of the wagon and went around to the front. Brother Simon stared after him for a long moment, then shrugged and lay down.

"Thou know what to do?" Simon asked the assistants.

"Fold your hands over your chest," Peter told him, lighting the candle at his head.

"Quiet now," Ruth warned him, lighting the candle at his feet.

There was a slight jerk, and the wagon started off down the road. Peter and Ruth mumbled mystical things and made strange passes with their hands over Brother Simon's body. Simon thought he heard a passing reference in Peter's mumble to a "Dr. Fell," and then to a "Father William," but he couldn't be sure.

After what seemed like hours to Brother Simon, but was actually slightly less than half an hour, the wagon stopped. Mordecai came around to the rear and dropped the tail hatch. "Get out," he said. "Remember, don't say anything until the candles are blown out."

With Mordecai in front, and Peter and Ruth carrying the candles on each side, Brother Simon was led out into the middle of a large field of high grass. The moon was almost full, and the distant trees and more distant hills were ghostly presences against the black night sky.

Mordecai kept going until he had located an ancient tree stump in the middle of the field. "Put your left hand over the stump," he directed Simon. "Now walk around the stump and chant, 'Warts stay when I go, keep away from me,' until you have completed fifty revolutions." He nodded at Peter and Ruth, who blew out the candles.

Brother Simon ran eagerly around the stump, chanting, "Warts stay when I go, keep away from me," at the top of his voice, while Mordecai and his assistants stood silently back and watched. After twenty or so revolutions, he slowed down a bit, and breathing became predominant over yelling. After thirty the chant became a mumble. But he easily completed the fifty turns, then stopped, looking questioningly at Mordecai.

"Come," Mordecai said, leading them all back to the road. He stood Brother Simon in the middle of the road and pointed him back the way they had come. "That way is your camp," he said. "Walk, do not run, back to camp. Chant your chant with every step. When you arrive in camp go right to sleep. Try not to talk to anyone until the morning."

"The warts," Brother Simon said, "they will be gone in the morning?"

"They will have started to disappear," Mordecai told him. "It will take a week before the last is gone. Use the potion. When it is gone, bury the pot. Go now. Do not look back."

Brother Simon, President of the United States, greatest tactician since Napoleon, turned and went off down the road. He did not look back.

> "Warts stay
>   when I go,"
>   he chanted,
> "keep away
>   from me."

Mordecai, Ruth, and Peter stood silently and watched the spiritual leader of the Simples until he was out of sight down the road, and his chant no longer carried back to them on the slight wind. Then they climbed back onboard the wagon and started north.

~~~~~~~~~~

22

They came upon Chicago Spaceport from the west, through La Salle. They were not alone from La Salle onward, for the townspeople were on the road also; on horses and mules and in wagons and surreys and carts, traveling in tight bunches toward the spaceport. The townspeople stopped in a field about a quarter mile from the main building complex, joining with many of their brethren there before them and many yet arriving from other directions. Several preachers had set up shop at different points on the field, and seemed to be taking turns haranguing the assembled gentlefolk.

Mordecai and company went on past the flock and up to the main gate, where they were halted by two young, nervous-looking guards. "You may let us pass," Mordecai told them firmly. "Despite our appearances, we are not of the hoi polloi. We have traveled a long way to get here, beginning in Palisades Enclave in the Duchy of California, and we're tired and dirty and would like to bathe. Has the Martian landed yet?"

"No, sir," one of the guards said, stepping aside and pulling open his half of the gate. "It's due later this afternoon." This convinced the other guard also, and he opened his half of the gate.

To their left as they entered was Chicago Control, the communications centers and computer information centers that had controlled a century of manned commercial spaceflights. To their right were the assembly buildings: huge cubical frameworks so large that the eye refused to accept the perspective until it noted the clouds drifting somewhere below the roofs. In front of them lay twenty-four square miles of concrete.

Dr. Pepperidge came down to meet them and was waiting in the doorway of the communications building when they parked the wagon. He shook hands enthusiastically with the three of them. "From California, eh?" he said. "You must be Mordecai; and of course Peter and Ruth. Welcome to Chicago. Your sense of timing is superb: two thousand miles and you arrive within four hours of the landing."

Peter's face assumed an expression of surprise. "How did you know?" he asked.

Pepperidge chuckled and slapped Peter on the back. "Don't worry," he said. "I assure you that you know far more magic than I. The gate guard told me. When you came through, he telephoned the center. And your wagon was the only one we were expecting from California; and you fit the descriptions we got over the radio; so I took a wild guess."

Pepperidge introduced himself and then pointed out a barracks area in a nearby building. "Find an empty room and take it over," he said. "Or rooms; as many as you like. The personnel quota this base was built to hold is far larger than the working contingent we have assembled here." He shook hands with them again. "I must go back upstairs," he said. "After you clean up, come join me. You wouldn't want to miss the landing."

"Not for the world," Mordecai said.

"Telephone," Peter said. "I'll have to get a look at that."

They found three empty rooms in the building, each with its own private bath. And the water was hot. Chicago Spaceport had energy to burn; at least until tomorrow, when the shuttle took off again and the scientists packed up and left for their various homes.

Pepperidge showed them around the com center when they returned. His job, he explained, was done. All he had to do now was sit around and worry and wait for something to go wrong.

The center was a giant room full of electronic consoles. Only one small corner of it, perhaps six desks, were manned and operative. "Much of it is redundant," Pepperidge explained, "and a lot of it is useless or pointless in this situation; for example, the monitoring links with the European and African ground stations. We don't know if the stations are even there anymore, and we have no way to find out. The amazing thing to us was how much of this equipment worked. I mean, we just put power to it, turned it on, and it worked."

"It's a lucky thing, isn't it?" Mordecai said.

"Well, we could have done a certain amount of improvisational repair, but by and large you're right," Pepperidge said.

A soft electronic beeper sounded and everyone in the room strove to look calm. "The shuttle should have just separated from the station," Pepperidge said. "We fed the last information into the ship's computer about twenty minutes ago. The tricky thing, you understand, is not landing; that ship should just about land itself. The trick is landing here."

"That runway looks pretty long to me," Peter said.

"Not from two hundred miles," Pepperidge. "And not at a landing speed of two hundred forty miles an hour. Remember, it's a dead-stick landing. The shuttle is in effect a very fast glider coming down; it has no power. Something like a ten-second difference in the time of the injection thrust—the one that starts him coming down—or a five per cent difference in its power would be enough to make him miss the whole state, not just this port."

"Well, was it right?" Ruth asked, looking around at all the somber-faced scientists gathered around their instruments.

"We don't know," Pepperidge said. "And we won't for ten minutes or so. The injection takes place on the other side of Earth, over India; and as I said, the relay stations are out."

"Wonderful," Peter said.

A runner approached and handed a note to Dr. Pepperidge. He opened it and read, then crumpled it and threw it in a corner. "Nothing much we can do about that," he said.

"What's the problem?" Mordecai asked.

"The locals are restless," Pepperidge told him.

"We know," Mordecai said. "We drove through a gathering of them."

"Well, now the gathering's moving this way. We're putting all available men at the gate or along the fence, but we'd hate to have to shoot any of the locals. It's not their fault, after all. The note said they'll be here in an hour if they keep moving."

"Probably a bit longer," Mordecai said. "They'll probably stop to bunch up and listen to speeches. I doubt if they have any clear idea of what to do when they get here."

"If we can keep them outside the fence for another four hours," Pepperidge said, "then it won't matter. When the shuttle takes off again the locals can rip up the base. It will have served its function."

"They'll want to rip you up too," Peter said.

"We're prepared for that," Pepperidge told him. "Enough of the flightline vehicles work to get us all across the field, and eight miles is a quite adequate head start. They'll stay here for quite a while burning and stoning all this beautiful equipment, anyway."

"How long will the shuttle be on the ground?" Mordecai asked.

"No one knows exactly," Pepperidge told him. "Turn-around time in the manuals was forty-eight hours, but that included checking a lot of stuff we're not equipped to check and a lot of stuff there's no point to checking because we couldn't replace it if it checked bad. We figure two hours to bolt on the solid-fuel boosters and somewhere between two and three hours to pump in the liquid fuel, if the pumps still work at the somewhat amazing capacities they're rated for. Since these operations can be accomplished simultaneously, a turn-around time of three hours seems possible. Isn't that a nice phrase: 'turn-around time'? Right out of the manuals."

"Isn't that overly dangerous?" Ruth asked. "I mean, if you check out something and it checks bad, and you can't replace it, shouldn't the Martian just stay here?"

"We're going to check the major systems," Pepperidge said. "If something is completely blown, if there's no chance of him getting off the ground, then Socrates will stay. But if there's any chance at all, he'll take it. His chance of staying alive on Earth once he cracks his helmet are less than one in ten."

"And he's doing it all for those animals marching for the gate," Peter said savagely. "They don't deserve it!"

Mordecai looked at him. "Perhaps," he said. "Should all of them die?"

"Probably not," Peter said. "There must be a few, you know, misled. But most of them—"

"Would you like to pick the ones to die?" Mordecai asked. Peter sighed an exasperated sigh. "Don't give me any of your philosophical arguments, Mordecai," he said. "Those people are marching on this place. And if killing any one or more of them would save Chicago Spaceport for the next few hours, and I had the means of doing it, I would."

"Aha, but what about when they're not marching; when they're back in their towns? Would you examine them and say, 'This one lives, but this one is no good and should die'?"

"It's a hypothetical question, and one I'll never have to consider," Peter said.

"Not until next month," Mordecai said, "when we start preparing the vaccine and looking for ways to inoculate a science-hating populace. It's going to be quite a problem."

"Chicago, this is the *Worden*, can you hear me? Chicago, this is Socrates Proudfoot in the shuttlecraft *Worden*, just coming over the west coast of North America. You should be able to hear me now. Can you hear me?" The voice, crackly and distant, sounded over the loudspeakers. The tone seemed curiously unemotional and detached to those listening in the com center. Socrates's Martian-taught astronaut objectivity was now alien to Earth.

"We hear you, Socrates, we hear you loud and clear. How was the blast?" It was Professor Jerob at the microphone.

"Right on time and perfect duration," Socrates's voice informed them. "If your computer's figures were right, I'm right on target."

"The radar should pick you up in a minute, if it's still working," Jerob called. "We'll give you a position check."

Ruth clutched at Peter's arm. "He's really made it," she said. "He's really here."

"You'll be able to tell your children you met a Martian," Peter said, out of a need for something to say.

Mordecai laid an arm on each of their shoulders. "You tell them," he said. "Tell them their mommy met a Martian, and that's why they're alive. It's enough to make me a religious man, if I weren't an atheist. How long till he's down?"

"Forty minutes," Pepperidge said. "Something like that."

"Position check on five," Jerob announced. He counted up to five and pushed a button, and a strange, multitoned beeping came from the speakers.

"What's that noise?" Peter asked.

"That's a computer talking to a computer," Pepperidge told him.

"All the wonders of the Golden Age," Peter said. "Telephones, spaceships, computers, hot water . . . it's almost beyond comprehension."

The runner came up to them again. "They're here," he said. "The first ones."

"What?" Pepperidge asked, distracted, "who?"

"The locals," the runner said. "The first ones are arriving at the main gate. The body of the mob is only a short distance behind." He paused for a few deep breaths. "They're not doing anything yet, just standing there and looking. The guards have locked the gate, of course."

"That note from Culver said an hour," Pepperidge complained.

"Yes, sir," the runner said. "He was wrong. I guess they were in a hurry." He ran off.

"Say," Peter said. "I thought you said there was a telephone."

"He didn't run all the way from the guard shack," Pepperidge told him. "Just up two flights of stairs. It's a voice-powered field phone from the guard shack at the gate to the guardroom downstairs."

"What are you going to do about the locals?" Mordecai asked.

"Not much we can do," Pepperidge said. "We certainly can't shoot them all. If they decide to break in, they'll succeed. Let's just hope they're happy yelling outside for the next few hours."

"What happens after the shuttle lands?" Peter asked. "I mean, what's your procedure?"

"First we wait for it to cool down," Pepperidge said. "Then we hook it onto the gantry, set it on its tail, and bolt those solid-fuel rockets to it. Then we wave good-bye. Let's hope that the locals are so impressed by the whole thing that they just sit there with their mouths open."

"Chicago, this is the *Worden*, glide correction made, touchdown in twenty-eight minutes."

"Where does it land?" Mordecai asked.

"West end of the field," Pepperidge said. "Then it rolls along for quite a way, and stops somewhere around here."

"I want to go watch," Peter said. "From outside."

"So do I," Mordecai agreed. Ruth nodded.

"I have to stay here," Pepperidge said. "They have to have some-one to pass notes to."

Mordecai, Peter, and Ruth left the communications building and walked out onto the field. The sun was in the west, and the great ribbon of concrete took on a reddish shimmer as it stretched out toward the sun. The yelling of the gathering crowd at the main gate was a low murmur in the distance behind them, strangely soothing as the waves of a distant sea or the squawking of a flock of nesting gulls on a far-off rock.

Then the thrumming of motors was added to the sounds, and a variety of vehicles appeared from behind a near building. There was an ambulance, and a jeep, and a pair of tank trucks with noz-zles on their hoods for spraying fire foam. They stayed lined up by the side of the building and waited.

And the sun went behind a cloud. And the sun came out from behind the cloud. And all was curiously still. And the waiting stretched on past endurance. And nothing was ever going to hap-pen. . . .

. . . and it came.

Suddenly, silently, it was there. A giant, boxy shape with in-credibly stubby wings, it dropped out of the sky as though thrown by a cosmic hand and disappeared into the sunlight reflecting off the runway.

And then nothing, as though it had never been.

And then a roar of wind, escaped from some distant hurricane.

And then it rushed into view at an impossible speed, grew in size at an incredible rate; a great silver barn with baby wings, vio-lently slowing as it approached. It passed them at an athlete's walk, slowed to a march, then to a crawl, then stopped reluctantly, looking as though it would like to go on.

The ambulance and tank trucks raced over to the shuttle and stopped at a respectful distance, waiting to see if they were needed. But the shuttle refused to catch fire, and the figure who appeared at the crew hatch in the bulky spacesuit appeared to have nothing broken.

The jeep towed a ramp over to the hatch and carefully pushed it into position. Then the Martian, slowly and ponderously, started down. By this time the people inside the com center were beginning to emerge from the building and gather outside the main door. A large, hand-lettered banner, reading WELCOME TO EARTH, was unrolled and held up by several undergraduates.

The Martian was helped into the back seat of the jeep and it was discovered that he couldn't sit down in the spacesuit. So he stood up, holding on to the roll bar, while the jeep was driven carefully over to the waiting area prepared for him. The area, laid out with a red carpet someone had found in supply, had a tank of clean oxygen for him to breathe and a chair for him to sit down on. Other amenities were thought of and discarded as being unsuitable for a man in a spacesuit. At the last moment someone had thought of bringing out a radio tuned to the communication channel, so they could talk to him without yelling into the helmet.

The Martian stepped out of the jeep onto the red carpet and stared at the crowd of Earthmen gathered around him, then he sat down. There was no applause, no waving, very few smiles. Everyone just stared somberly at Socrates for a moment, then at one another, then went off to start their assigned duties for the second half of the job.

Dr. Pepperidge took up the microphone. "Socrates?"

"Yes?" The Martian's voice echoed tinnily out of the tiny speaker.

"Are you all right? Do you need anything?"

"I'm fine," Socrates said. "My cargo is in a large metal box inside the hatch. Send a couple of men over to get it down; you wouldn't want to drop it now."

Pepperidge nodded to the men in the jeep and they turned it around and headed back to the shuttle. "Welcome to Earth," Pepperidge said, then shrugged. "I should have prepared a speech or something, I guess. I can't think of anything adequate to say."

"I have become unaccustomed to speech," Socrates said. "Just let me look around and gather what impressions I can. How long will I be here?"

"They have to hook your ship up to the gantry and stand it on end," Pepperidge said. "Then bolt the solid boosters to it and pump the fuel and oxygen in. Maybe four hours, maybe twelve. Then we wait up to another two hours for the right moment to launch."

"I haven't that much oxygen," Socrates said.

"That tank behind you was filled from the liquid-oxygen plant, so it's safe," Pepperidge said. "You can hook up to it whenever you like."

Socrates nodded. "Very good," he said, then leaned back in his chair as best he could with the tanks on his back, content to wait and watch.

Mordecai, who had come up to Dr. Pepperidge during this conversation, tapped Pepperidge on the shoulder. "Do you notice anything?" he asked.

Pepperidge looked annoyed. "What sort of anything?"

"The natives have grown silent."

Pepperidge considered. "You could hear them before? I was inside."

"A steady roar," Mordecai told him.

"What do you suppose it means?" Pepperidge asked.

Mordecai shook his head. "I couldn't guess," he said. "They could be so impressed by the landing that they're going to sit quietly and watch for the next week, or they could be gathering courage to do almost anything."

"Well, we'd better be prepared," Pepperidge said. He gave instructions to the men who had driven the tank trucks, and they sprinted for the rear of the building.

"What is all this about?" Socrates asked over his tinny speaker. "What natives?"

"The people of the local towns," Pepperidge explained. "They, and most of their kith throughout the world, hold science responsible for the Death."

"So I had heard," Socrates said. "I didn't believe it, really."

"Oh, it's true," Mordecai said. "A mob of them are gathered outside the spaceport now, trying to decide what to do about us."

The jeep scuttled back toward them from the spacecraft, with a large metal box sitting on the back seat.

"By the way," Mordecai asked Pepperidge, "where'd you get the tires? I thought they'd all deteriorated to the point where they wouldn't hold air."

"They have," Pepperidge told him. "We came up with a bunch of solid rubber tires in storage here. They're a little off round in spots, but they work fine."

All at once a full-throated roar sounded from the mob beyond the gate. It began and ended so precisely that it might have been led by practiced cheerleaders. Then it came again, and again, as though voiced by one throat.

"Get out of here," Pepperidge told the jeep driver. "Get across the field to where the wagons are parked. Get that box on a wagon and get it to the university as quickly as possible. Shoot anyone who tries to stop you."

"Yes, sir," the driver said, and he and his companion started back across the field, away from the mob.

"I never thought I'd tell anyone that," Pepperidge said.

Mordecai turned to Peter and Ruth, who were standing a little way off. "You'd better get to the wagon," he said, "and head out after the jeep. We'd better try to save the wagon, we may need it."

"Right," Peter said.

Ruth walked over to the Martian and looked at him through the helmet. "My name is Ruth," she said.

"I'm Socrates," he said. "Socrates Proudfoot."

"Thank you," she said.

"You're welcome," he said.

She extended her hand, and he took it in his thick glove. After a moment she turned and ran back to Peter, and they started for the wagon.

The roaring from the gate continued, and a runner approached Pepperidge from the guardhouse. "The gate says they're breaking in," he said. "What should they do?"

Pepperidge sat down. "Tell them to get the hell out of there," he said. "There's nothing they can do."

The runner raced back.

Three blue and white buses came around the building and stopped by the main doors. The first of the mob came into view around a distant building, running toward the silver cylinders of the booster rockets.

Pepperidge looked at Mordecai and then at Socrates. "I have to evacuate the gantry," he said.

"I don't take off?" Socrates asked.

"You don't take off," Mordecai told him.

Pepperidge took up the handset of a field phone that had been set up for him and cranked the bell. "Evacuate," he said into it.

A siren sounded. One of the buses headed to the gantry. The other two began taking on people from the com center.

Socrates released the catches and turned and removed his helmet. He threw it aside and took a few deep breaths of Earth air. "Help me out of this suit," he said.

The bus pulled away from the gantry just before the mob reached it. Half the mob split off and headed for the shuttle.

Ten minutes later, as their bus caught up with the wagon toward the far end of the field, a brilliant fireball leaped toward the sky behind them, searing the eyes of all who were looking back. Another thirty seconds and the sound wave hit, like the hand of an invisible giant slamming against the bus.

Mordecai turned to Socrates, sitting next to him. "Welcome to Earth," he said.